First published in Great Britain in 2013 by
Simon and Schuster UK Ltd
A CBS COMPANY

Originally published in the USA in 2012 by Simon Spotlight,
an imprint of Simon & Schuster Children's Division, New York.

Copyright © 2012 by Simon and Schuster, Inc.
Text by Elizabeth Doyle Carey. Design by Laura Roode.

Simon & Schuster UK Ltd
1st Floor, 222 Gray's Inn Road, London WC1X 8HB

Simon & Schuster Australia, Sydney
Simon & Schuster India, New Delhi

A CIP catalogue record for this book
is available from the British Library.

PB ISBN 978-1-47111-636-0
EBook ISBN 978-1-47111-637-7

1 3 5 7 9 10 8 6 4 2

Printed and bound by CPI Group (UK) Ltd, Croydon, CR0 4YY

www.simonandschuster.co.uk
www.simonandschuster.com.au

The
Cupcake Diaries

emma,
Smile and Say 'Cupcake!'

Coco Simon

SIMON AND SCHUSTER

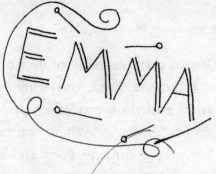

CHAPTER 1

On Pins and Needles

I woke up extra early this Saturday morning to ice the mini cupcakes I was delivering to our number-one client, Mona, at The Special Day bridal salon. Well, the truth was, icing wouldn't take long, but I wanted to wash and set my hair in my mum's big rollers before I went to the bridal salon. I would be modelling today for Mona's clients, and I wanted to try a new hairstyle and see what everyone at the shop thought.

It's kind of crazy how I started modelling for Mona. One Saturday morning I was making a regular cupcake delivery to the shop (my friends and I in the Cupcake Club have a cupcake business, and Mona buys cupcakes from us for her Saturday brides each week), and an important mystery client was there for an early showing of dresses. It turned out to be Romaine Ford, our only hometown celebrity, and I ended up modelling junior brides-maid dresses for her because there was no one else available. Meeting Romaine Ford and everything that came after that was the most exciting part of my life yet.

Since then, I've been modelling for Mona about once or twice a month for trunk shows, which is when specialty designers bring in their line for the day. It's fun. I get to dress up and sometimes have my hair styled (no makeup, though! It could ruin the dresses!) and hang out in a totally girlie environment for the morning, away from my three smelly brothers. Best of all, Mona pays me.

So this morning I showered, then put on my fancy jeans and a pretty turtleneck jumper, some tiny pearl stud earrings, and a belt. Then I rolled my hair and forgot all about it for a while as I finished up the cupcakes. Well, until my brother Matt walked into the kitchen and fell down on the floor laughing. I guess I looked pretty funny with my hair all in rollers, but there are times like these when I really wish I had a sister. Anyway, it only took about half an hour to ice and pack the cupcakes since they're minis, which are not much wider than a coin. Mona loves them. Brides are always on diets, so ~~they're~~ hungry, which makes them cranky. These cupcakes are so tiny, no one can resist, and she says they make cranky brides friendlier. Isn't that funny?

Afterwards, I ran the blow-dryer over my curlers to really set my hair, then I unpinned the rollers and swung my head from side to side. My hair is a very yellow blonde on top, from the sun, but underneath it's a much darker shade. The curls made the colours all swirly and mixed together, and the style gave me a lot of height. I looked two inches taller! I laughed at the sight of it. It might be too much, but who cared? It was just an experiment, anyway. Well, my mum might care. She's always concerned about being "age appropriate."

My mum called up from the kitchen that we had to go or I'd be late, so I flipped off the bathroom light and took the stairs down, two at a time. As I swung around the banister and into the kitchen, my mum turned around and then did a double take.

"Oh, Emma! Your hair looks gorgeous!" she said with a gasp.

I grinned. "Thanks! You don't think it's too much?"

My mum laughed. "Well, maybe for football practice or something, but under the circumstances,

3

I think it will be a huge success!" She smoothed her own perky blonde ponytail and laughed again, looking down at her tracksuit. "I am feeling very underdressed!"

"You look great, Mama," I said, calling her by my private baby name for her. "You're the prettiest mum in school." I grabbed my jacket off the hook in my locker in the mudroom, stepped over about five piles of sweaty boys' sporting goods, and headed out to the car.

"Thank you, lovebug, you do say the sweetest things, even if they're not always true!"

At The Special Day, Mona and her assistants were bustling around getting things set up for the day's trunk show.

The Special Day is just what you would imagine if you were trying to picture the most awesome, over-the-top, bridal shop. It's like a magical castle, and someday that's where I want to buy my wedding dress. First of all, outside the store they have beautiful green trees, and topiaries in white wooden flower boxes, and a pretty white awning with white lanterns hanging on either side of the door. It looks like something from movies I've seen of Paris. Then, inside is white, white, white everywhere. A boy couldn't last one minute in there without ruining something, I tell you. There are thick white pile carpets, which make it really quiet; superplush white sofas and chairs that you sink into; low white marble coffee tables where tea is served in fine white china; and everywhere are white boxes of white Kleenex, because everyone cries when women try on wedding dresses. Once, I even saw Mona tear up when a young woman with cancer came in to try on her dress. She was bald from her treatment, but very brave and getting healthier, and Mona cried when she saw her in her beautiful dress.

Today, Mona's main assistant, Patricia, came striding over to help me with my cupcake carriers. "Oh, Emma! Your hair! You look incredible!" said Patricia.

I smiled. "Thanks. It was just an experiment."

"Well, it looks wonderful. Mona! Come see Emma's new hairstyle!"

Mona looked up from the rack of dresses she was arranging, and I saw her tilt her head and squint at me. "Emma!" she cried. (Mona is really dramatic, by the way. Did I mention that?) She raced across the store towards me, her arms outstretched. "Darling! You look divine! Simply divine!" She had her

5

hands on my arms, and now she pulled me in for a European-style two-cheek kiss. I laughed.

Mona said, "Oh, Patricia, isn't she divine?"

Smiling, Patricia nodded and added, "Divine!"

(Did I mention that "divine" is Mona's favourite word?) But now Mona stopped gushing over me and patted her severe black bun. "Patricia!" she snapped, all business now. "I have an idea!"

"Yes, Mona? What is it?" asked Patricia. Patricia is very patient, but I guess I don't need to mention that either.

Mona circled me, looking at my new hair with her arms folded, tapping her chin, slightly bent at the waist. "Mm-hmm. Mm-hmm. Yes. Yes!" After what felt like an eternity, she looked up at Patricia with a gleam in her eye. "Call Emma's mother and ask if we can photograph her today, and if so, could we use it in the paper. Then if she says yes, call Joachim and get him over here on the double. I'd like to run another ad!"

I raised my eyebrows at Patricia and she raised hers back at me, and we smiled like coconspirators. An ad?! Holy smokes! *Wait until I tell my friends,* was all I could think! I prayed my mum said yes. Sometimes my parents can be funny about stuff like that – they always are nice when people tell them

6

I'm pretty, like if we're out to dinner or something, but they always tell me after that looks don't last and that schoolwork and teamwork are more important than appearances. I know what they mean, but I still like it when people say I'm pretty. Especially because I don't think I'm pretty all the time; only when I try a little and, like, wear something fancy or do my hair. Otherwise I think I just look normal.

I went with Patricia to sort through the dresses I'd wear today while she dialled my mum's mobile on the cordless phone. Today's dresses were by Jaden Sacks, a famous designer from New York City. The line is superchic and exclusive. She usually only sells in her boutique on Madison Avenue. I know this because Mona told me the week before. She was very excited to be able to carry the dresses in the shop. The junior bridesmaid dresses were gorgeous, made of incredible materials – thick, slippery satin that pooled in my hand and slid through my fingers like quicksilver; pleated sheer silk so light and thin, it was like candy floss on my skin; and lace that was somehow detailed and fancy on one side but cotton soft on the underside so it buffered me from the scratchiness of the stitching. The designs were simple – fashion forward but not tacky or overdone. Jaden Sacks is famous for using the finest supplies and craftspeople. Mona also told me that, but I looked it up on the Internet, too. Her dresses for brides are not traditional puffy "wedding cakes" with lots of layers, but rather columns or sheaths or mermaids with trains. Very glamorous and understated. Her dresses for junior bridesmaids don't really look like bridesmaids dresses. They aren't too poufy or lacy or anything, and they don't look like mini brides, but they still look what my mum would call "age appropriate." Which is good, because when it comes to modelling, my mum is all over being age appropriate. Mona has to show Mum all the dresses I'll wear beforehand, so she can okay them. It's kind of crazy. I mean, how can a bridesmaid dress be too sexy? But Mona says you'd be surprised.

Patricia whispered to me as she waited for my mum to pick up the phone, telling me that Mona was hoping Jaden Sacks might consider letting her carry the dresses for good, selling the line as a regular attraction at the store. Mona had already run a number of ads in the local paper about today's trunk show, and she was expecting a big crowd – not just brides but local fashionistas who were curious to see the exclusive line on their home turf. (I already knew that one of my best friends, Mia, and her mum, Mrs Valdes, who were major fashionistas and were clients of Mona's, were coming today to inspect the line and cheer on Mona. I couldn't wait to tell Mia about the potential ad!)

I could hear Patricia speaking to my mum.

"Oh, Mrs Taylor! Hi! It's Patricia at The Special Day! No, everything's fine. She's here. Everything is wonderful." There was a pause. "No! The hair is divine! That's actually why I'm calling you. Mona loved it so much that she had an idea to shoot photos of Emma today to run in an ad in the paper, and she wanted to know if that would be okay with you. We'd pay her extra, of course." There was another pause. "Yes, I totally understand. No, it's not a problem at all. Okay, talk soon. Bye!" Patricia clicked the off button on the phone and set the receiver on the bench in the large fitting room. I waited for Patricia to give me the scoop. When she didn't immediately say anything, I had to ask.

"What did she say?!" I couldn't contain my excitement any longer.

"She said it sounded like fun, but she wanted to talk it over with your father before she gave her permission."

"What? That is such a bummer!" I complained. I knew it was babyish, but I didn't care. How could

9

my mum even think of saying no to an opportunity like this? My mum was protective, but oh boy, my dad was even more protective of me. There's no way he'd say yes.

"Hey, modelling is a big deal," Patricia reminded me gently. "You're talking about putting your photo out there for all the world to see. It might seem like fun for you, but maybe your parents are worried it will give you an image that's not consistent with what they want for you. I completely respect your mother's response. Trust me" – Patricia rolled her eyes – "in the fashion business you get plenty of mothers who are just the opposite – pushing their very young daughters at you, willing to sell their souls to the devil just to make some money off their child's looks before they change or get braces or whatever. It's a tough business."

"One ad doesn't mean I'm in the modelling business!" I protested.

Patricia smiled a wry smile. "It might," she said. "I'm calling Joachim, just in case, and telling him to stand by." She grabbed my hand and squeezed, then handed me my first dress and motioned that she was leaving.

I beamed at Patricia and held up my crossed fingers as she left. Then I began to get ready. I hate changing in front of other people, so Mona got me a slip to wear under the dresses – it's kind of like a long stretchy nude-coloured camisole, and it makes me feel more comfortable, in case someone accidentally barges in. But Patricia always leaves me alone to get the slip on and get started, and she calls in to make sure I'm ready before she comes back. We have a good routine now, and we totally get each other. It's kind of weird to think that one of my friends could be forty years older than me and working full-time in a bridal salon, but I'd have to say that's the case with me and Patricia.

The first Jaden Sacks dress was just so gorgeous. It had a high square neckline and what Patricia called "tulip" sleeves, which were capped kind of midway down my upper arm with overlapping petals of fabric. Then a high plain waist with a pale blue ribbon to define it, and a floor-length skirt of satin that swished heavily as I walked. The best part was it had a very light tulle underskirt in a pale blue that matched the ribbon and peeked out only when I moved. I loved it.

I called Patricia, and she came back in, the phone pressed to hear ear, nodding. Whoever she was talking to wouldn't let her get a word in edgewise. I hoped it wasn't my mum!

I watched her face in the mirror as she bent her knees and clutched the receiver between her shoulder and chin so she could tie my ribbon with both hands. Then she leaned to the side to look at me in the mirror and gave me two thumbs-up and a wink. That meant I looked great. But who was on the phone?

"Uh-huh. Yes. Yes. Okay. Right." Patricia was nodding again.

I knitted my eyebrows together and mouthed, *My mum?* I was on pins and needles waiting to hear. But Patricia shook her head and covered the receiver with her hand. *Joachim,* she mouthed, and she rolled her eyes for the second time today. "Right. Well, listen, Joachim, that's all great. I think your vision sounds wonderful, and we will have all the snacks on hand that you requested, as well as a space roped off for your shoot, and total privacy. Yes. I understand it will be a Sunday rate because it is so last-minute. I will confirm as soon as I hear back from the model. Thank you."

Patricia sighed a deep sigh and sat down heavily on the bench. "This is going to be a really long day," she said.

designed by
JAYDEN SACKS!

CHAPTER 2

American Beauty

$\mathcal{M}$y parents were killing me! It was midmorning, and they still hadn't called Patricia back yet. Meanwhile, the shop was packed, and Mona had made one of the assistants hide the cupcakes in the back because all the people who came to just look at the dresses were eating them, and there weren't going to be any left for the scheduled brides who might actually buy dresses. I knew that my best friend Alexis, who was the business brains of our Cupcake Club, would die if she thought we were missing a business opportunity, so I borrowed Patricia's phone and called her house to see if she could rush over a few dozen more minis and some business cards to lay around. She said she would and that she'd call Katie and Mia, the other Cupcakers, to come and help if they could, just to speed things along. She hoped to be there by midafternoon. Feeling proud of that accomplishment, I raced off to change again.

Mona wanted me to rotate looks every half hour, working my way through the six junior bridesmaid dresses and then taking a lunch break and starting over. By eleven thirty I was starting to fade. I put on the final dress before lunch. It was an Asian-influenced dress Patricia called a "cheongsam." It was made of white satin, with white dragons embroidered all over it, and it had short sleeves and a high Mandarin collar all piped in white. The dress was very fitted, with a diagonal flap across the front that closed with small Chinese rope catches called "frogs." I loved the look of it. It would be really cool to have a Chinese wedding, Patricia and I decided, with Chinese food and a tea ceremony and fireworks! As Patricia fastened the final frog, the store's phone rang and Patricia answered it. "Hello! It's The Special Day!"

I was adjusting my dress, looking in the mirror, when she said, "Hi, Mrs Taylor. Of course, she's right here." And she handed me the phone. "It's your mum. I'll be at the front desk when you're finished." She left, closing the door discreetly behind her.

14

I wished I could sit, but the tight dress made it impossible. Mentally, I scratched the idea of the Chinese wedding. The clothes were too snug! I leaned against the wall instead. "Hi, Mum. Can I do it?!" I asked impatiently.

"Hi, honey. Your dad and I have had a long talk, and we think there are pros and cons to being in the ad—"

"But, Mum!" I interrupted, ready to unleash the torrent of reasons I'd been stewing about all morning.

"No interrupting, Emma. Let me say my piece," said my mother in the stern voice she mostly uses on the boys. When I hear it, I know she means business.

"Fine," I muttered, feeling more in control for saying it, but also hoping she wouldn't hear me or I'd get in trouble for being fresh.

"Your father and I are nervous about the idea of you being in an ad. We are not sure this is a route you should be taking in life. As you know, we think your looks are a wonderful gift, but they are just one of many gifts you have that you need to develop. Your father and I also aren't crazy about the whole beauty culture in this country; we see eating disorders and masses of makeup and insecurity and

15

competition among young girls, and it is just not healthy. You need to keep a level head. In addition, we don't love the idea of your photo being out there for all the world to see. Some weirdo might clip it out and hang it on his wall, and that gives us the creeps."

"Mum!" I protested. But that *was* kind of creepy, now that she mentioned it.

She continued. "We also want you to know that being photographed by professionals is hard work. If you agree to do this for Mona, there is to be no eye rolling or sulking or slouching or all the many things you pull when we try to take a family photo at home."

"But that's totally different!" I cried.

"I know, but it's something to bear in mind. Modelling is hard work," she repeated.

"I know." I sighed in exasperation, looking down at my seat-preventing dress.

There was a pause on the other end of the phone.

"Mum?" I asked.

"Yes. So, if you understand all those things, and more, and are still interested, Dad and I consent to having you photographed for an ad – just this once. Okay?"

I couldn't believe it!

"Yay! Thanks, Mum! Thank you so much! It will be great. Don't worry!"

"And Dad will be there to supervise."

"Wait, *what?*"

"Just have Patricia call him with the timing. Good-bye!" And she hung up.

I stared at the receiver in shock. My *dad* was coming to The Special Day? To supervise me?

OMG!

At twelve I took off the Chinese dress with relief and went to a Mexican fast-food restaurant in the food court to grab a quick bite of lunch. After I ate my burrito, I still had twenty minutes of my hour break time left, so I strolled to the bookstore and went to the beauty section. They had books on modelling there, and I wanted to flip through one or two before I got back to the store.

I had to think about the whole modelling thing in a new way now.

Before, it had been the one lucky occasion when I'd modelled for Romaine. Then, when Mona had asked me back, it had seemed like a fun way to earn money. Since my family is per-petually short on cash (especially me), I always like

17

the opportunity to make a little more. I'm not a future CEO or anything like Alexis, but I do have a little neighbourhood dog-walking business, and the Cupcake Club, of course, and lately, the trunk-show modelling. It's a nice, small, steady stream of income, but it's not life-changing money. It just means I can eat at the food court at the mall instead of bringing a P-B-and-J sandwich from home, for example.

But I knew that being in ads could actually earn you some real money. Not just eight or ten dollars an hour.

I selected a book called *World Models*, and I flipped through it. It showed models in their home towns (and cities and villages), dressed in wild fashion couture that made them look really out of place, like freaks. I guess that was the point. I sighed and replaced it and then selected another.

This one was called *American Beauties*. It was organised by state, and I flipped through Alaska (a surprising number of models come from there, as it turns out) and on to Arizona, California and Connecticut before I realised most of these models were just a little bit older than me (sixteen, seventeen and eighteen years old) or had started out in the business as kids, like me (or even younger, I guess). In the interviews alongside the big photos, the models talked about how they were discovered. You can't believe how many of them were discovered at their local shopping centre!

Intrigued, I looked around to see if there were any modelling scouts nearby, but everyone seemed pretty engrossed in their books. I rifled through the pages one last time and was about to shut the book when a highlighted quote in bright orange type from a Native American model (from Arizona) jumped out at me. It said, "Just don't let them steal your soul."

Okaaay! I thought. Now that's another creepy thing to think about! I shut the book and reshelved it, then stood up to head back to work. My friends would be there soon, and I was looking forward to seeing them. My dad would be there after that, and I was *not* looking forward to seeing him. As I walked back to the shop, I played out different scenarios in my mind of my dad at The Special Day. In one, he was like a bull in a china shop, knocking into things and spilling tea on the sofa and generally embarrassing me. In another, he was his usual fun self, chatting everyone up and asking his or her life stories and generally embarrassing me. In yet another, he was falling asleep on the sofa and snoring, like he does in front of college football games on TV, and generally embarrassing me. Are you getting the idea here? I knew embarrassment was in store for me no matter what. Back at the shop I ran to the ladies' room to wash my hands (clean hands are a must at a bridal salon – most of the employees wear white gloves) and to make sure my face didn't have random flecks of salsa still on it.

Then I found Patricia and confirmed the lineup of my next round of dresses, and I went to change.

"Yoo-hoo!" I heard as I pulled the tulip-sleeved gown back over my head. It was Alexis!

"In here! Let me just get this dress on and you can come in. Was Mona surprised about the cupcakes?" I asked through the closed door.

"Yeah. I told her they were on the house if she'd let us put out our cards, and she said great. Hey, it's packed out there, by the way. If we don't get at least one job out of this, I'll be shocked," Alexis said happily.

I smiled. Alexis is happiest when growing a business.

"Okay, ready! Come in! And you can tie me," I called. Patricia was so busy, Alexis could easily do the styling work for me.

"Wow! Your hair really looks amazing!" said

Alexis as she entered the changing room.

After looking at myself in the mirror all day, I had forgotten about the curls. "Thanks!" I said, patting my hair. "Will you tie me, please?"

Alexis kept staring at me in the mirror as she deftly tied the bow. "Really, I can't get over it. It's like you're a different person," she said. "You look like a model!"

"I am!" I laughed. "And guess what?" I said, spinning around to face Alexis. "Mona asked me if she could put me in an ad in the paper, and my parents said yes! We're having a photo shoot later today with a professional photographer, who sounds cuckoo, by the way!"

Alexis's jaw dropped. "OMG. Do you know how much money you can make doing that?"

I laughed again. "Leave it to you, Miss CEO, to think of the money."

Alexis furrowed her brow. "Well, what else would you think of? It's not like it's fun."

"I think it will be. I think the photo shoot will be really glamorous, and I think it will be unbelievable to have a few people see my photo in the paper."

"I don't know . . . But, anyway, it's great news and I'm so happy for you!" said Alexis, and she grabbed me in a big hug. "I know a supermodel!"

"The dress!"

"Oops. Sorry. I guess this dress wasn't made to withstand BFFs," she said with a giggle.

"I guess not. . ." I giggled too. "Hey, are the others here?"

"Yeah, come on. They won't believe your hair when they see it. I can't wait!" Alexis grabbed my hand and pulled me out of the dressing room, through the throngs of women in the shop, searching for our friends.

Along the way, a couple of ladies noticed my dress, "Ooh, isn't that exquisite?" said one.

And "That is a gorgeous dress!" said another.

"Alexis!" I protested. They were the people I was meant to be talking to right now. They were the potential clients, and I was there to sell. But Alexis was whisking me right past them. "Alexis! Stop!" I cried, finally yanking back my hand.

She turned around, and her smile faded. "What?" she asked, seeing my worried face.

"I'm working. And you just dragged me past two women who were interested in my dress. You can't do that. I have to go back there and tell them about it."

Alexis looked perplexed. "Oh. Right. Okay."

"I'm sorry. It's not that I don't want to see the others; it's just that Mona is paying me to do this. Can you just find Mia and Katie and bring them to me instead?" I felt bossy and horrible, killing Alexis's enthusiasm like that. Guilt settled heavily in the pit of my stomach.

"Okay," said Alexis again. Then she smiled. "You go back, and I'll come find you when I get the others." If anyone got the fact that I was working and making money, it was Alexis.

I turned back to find the interested women. Pasting a gracious smile on my face, I walked back very slowly, making eye contact with everyone, just as Patricia and Mona had taught me at my first trunk show. That's one of the ways people know you're an employee, and then they feel you're approachable and they can ask you questions about your dress. Part of my job is to know the designer's name, the dress's style name, and the price of each and every dress I wear. Just enough info so that the clients can follow up with Mona for more specifics, like sizing and lead time (that's how long it takes to have the dress made).

I found the first woman standing with her friend, and I began chatting with them, telling them all about the dress. They loved it and were pretty impressed by all the information I had. (I couldn't resist throwing in the term "tulip sleeve." What can I say?) Then I moved on to the other interested woman and let her look at the seams and feel the fabric and generally judge the quality of the dress, which she found "impeccable." Not that I was surprised. All the Jaden Sacks dresses are impeccable, which made it fun to wear them and have clients be impressed.

When she'd finished, I turned and went looking for someone else to show the dress to. But suddenly the crowd parted, and Katie and Mia and Alexis appeared. I was happy to see them, even if I was self-conscious about socialising on the job. Katie and Mia squealed about my hair and the news about the photo shoot, and Katie said, "Oh, Emma, I'm so jealous! I can't believe you're a model and you're going to be in the paper. You're famous! You're like Maple Grove's next Romaine Ford!"

I had to really laugh at that one. "Romaine Ford is a talented dancer, singer and actress, Katie. I am just a clothes hanger!"

"It's a big deal!" said Mia, whose mum is a fashion stylist. "I've been to modelling shoots in the city with my mum lots of times, and let me tell you, it is no picnic. Those hot lights, the cranky photo-

24

graphers, the uncomfortable clothes with pins poking you, the competitive models who all want your spot . . . It is a J–O–B, for real!"

"Yeah," I agreed, but I could feel my brow furrowing as it always does when I'm nervous. Well, how bad could one photo shoot be, anyway?

Mia's mum appeared then. "Oh, Emma, you look lovely, *mi amor*!"

I smiled. "Thanks, Mrs Valdes."

"I love that dress, and I simply adore your hair like that!"

"Mum, Emma's going to be in a print ad for the store. Isn't that great?" said Mia.

"Wow, that's spectacular! I can't wait to see it! I hope they're paying you well. It's hard work," she said, leaning in so no one else could hear.

I grinned. "That's what I hear."

She rolled her eyes. Then she said, "All right, chicas, Emma is working, so we'd better be running along now. Good-bye, darling. Have a great time. I can't wait to see your ad!" Mrs Valdes blew me a kiss, and they left.

I watched them walk away until the crowd swallowed them, and I couldn't help but wonder where they were all going and what they were going to do. It would be fun to just put on jeans and hang out with them. Maybe they'd shop around the shops for a while; Mrs Valdes is the best mum to go to the mall with, because she loves clothing and loves to shop (unlike my mum). She has an eye for the inexpensive item that can really tie everything together. Or maybe they'd head to the movies and then the new milkshake place, and there would be cute boys there to flirt with. I felt lonely and left out and suddenly wished I was going with them. And yet I had two more hours of modelling and then the shoot.

"Emma!" Patricia was calling me, and I snapped to. "Time to put on the next look, please!"

"Right," I said, and I hurried back to the changing room alone.

CHAPTER 3

Makeup Session

At least my father looked good when he showed up. He is a good-looking guy – tall, burly and athletic, with bright blue eyes, dark hair and a smile that makes the corners of his eyes crinkle up in a cute way. Today he had changed out of his customary Saturday T-shirt–and–shorts sports attire (he plays football in an adult rec league and coaches at least one of my brothers' sports teams each season), and he was wearing what I think of as his out-to-Sunday-dinner attire: brown cords, loafers and a striped button-down shirt under a navy blue zip-neck jumper. He had the Sunday paper under his arm (we get most of it delivered with the Saturday paper; don't ask!), and he looked ready to settle in for the rest of the day.

Mona was impressed, I could tell, and this made me relax a little. Maybe he wouldn't embarrass me in some awful unpredictable way. She fussed over him and brought him a cup of coffee and a plate of mini cupcakes and then told him she and her staff were at his beck and call and not to hesitate if he needed anything.

"I can see why you like coming here!" he said to me with a laugh. "I'm thinking of spending every Saturday here from now on!"

"Dad, please!"

"Just kidding, angel. How was your morning?"

He had been surprised when he arrived and saw my hair, because he hadn't seen it earlier. When he recovered from the surprise, he told me how pretty it looked, even if it was a little done up for the jeans and turtleneck I had changed back into by then.

As we waited, a tiny, skinny man in a black leather jacket and black leather jeans came to the door. He had a faux hawk of jet-black hair, and big black combat boots on. I could see my dad's radar go up, and he sat up a little straighter, alert. The guy looked like trouble, and suddenly, I was really glad my dad was there.

But then Mona said, "Oh, here's Joachim! Late as usual!"

I know my jaw dropped, and I turned to my dad in shock. "That's the photographer," I whispered breathlessly.

"That scary-looking little dude?" My dad shook his head like he couldn't believe what he was hearing and what he was seeing. "But where is his . . ."

Suddenly, three other people struggled into view, carrying all sorts of metal strongboxes and lights and cables. My dad and I looked at each other again, and we smiled. "I guess that answers your question, right?" I said.

To see the next half hour unfold was mesmerising. Mona was bossing Joachim and his team around, cautioning them not to touch anything, not to stain anything, to be careful of their equipment marking anything. And Joachim was pushing back, asking where things would go otherwise and how could he work like this, and at the same time barking orders at his staff. It was like a standoff. I wondered who would win and at the same time, I fervently hoped I wouldn't be the biggest loser of the day. If they treated one another like this under these circumstances, I could only imagine where I'd fall in the pecking order!

My dad settled in with his newspaper (Mona had an assistant drape a white sheet over the sofa, so the newsprint didn't stain it; how that could happen, I don't know) and he seemed happy as a clam, but I was growing more and more nervous by the minute. All this lighting? All this equipment? Computers? Backdrops on rolls? All for one photo of me, a girl who had never posed professionally before? I kept gulping as each new component was put into place.

Finally, Patricia and one of Joachim's assistants, a goth-looking girl who was also all in black, came to get me ready. Patricia introduced me to Serena and said Serena'd spruce up my hair and do my makeup.

My dad, who had been totally checked out, suddenly came alive from behind his paper.

"No makeup," he said.

Patricia and Serena paused and looked at each other. "Excuse me?" Patricia asked politely.

My dad lowered his paper and looked at them from over his reading glasses. "No makeup. I don't want you to glam her up and have her looking like an adult. She's still a child."

Patricia smiled. "Mr Taylor, I promise you that the kind of makeup we are considering will be very sparingly applied and only used to enhance Emma's natural beauty. She will be totally recognisable as your daughter."

Serena spoke up, much more polite than I would have expected a goth to be. "It's just that with the lighting and with the transition from a computer image to the printed page, certain features tend to wash out; we need to prevent that from happening. We can do it on the front end with some inexpensive makeup or on the back end with expensive retouching in the studio. You'll see her before we shoot. And we'll let you see the pictures, and then you'll understand."

My father mulled this over. "I promised her mother no makeup. Let's see how she looks when she comes back out, and we'll make any adjustments if we need to, okay?"

I rolled my eyes, mortified by how clueless my father was, and followed Serena and Patricia to the changing room. Well, at least he didn't say no.

Inside, an entire makeup bench had been set up, with two high stools facing each other and very bright lighting. There was a makeup box – one of the black strongboxes I'd seen the team carrying in – opened on the table and a whole miniflight of "stairs" was expanded out of it, each with a dozen makeup colours on it. There were makeup brushes and hairspray bottles, cotton balls, a hairdryer, nail polish – everything you could think of.

31

"Now, dress first, do you think, or makeup?" asked Patricia.

"Makeup," said Serena definitively.

She gestured to the chair, and I clambered aboard. It was high, and my legs dangled frantically until I found a perch to settle them on.

Serena looked at me very closely, tilting her head this way and that, adjusting the light, then touching my chin and tipping it here and there. It was kind of weird, like I wasn't even a person but just a face with nothing behind it.

She pulled away and squinted at me, then she said, "Eyes." And with that, she got to work.

I glanced at Patricia, who was standing a little behind Serena, watching with a very serious look on her face. She smiled encouragingly at me, but her face instantly resumed its serious look, which wasn't exactly comforting. I felt like I was being operated on.

"Close," commanded Serena, and I closed my eyes. This part was easy, so far, if a little scary.

I felt Serena wiping something wet on my eyelids, and my eyes started to flutter. Serena sighed and stopped. I opened my eyes and found her staring at me with a kind of an annoyed look on her face.

"Aren't you a pro?" she asked.

"I . . . What?" I wasn't sure what to say.

Patricia leaned in and said, "This is her first photo shoot. She does in-store modelling for us, no makeup. Why don't you just talk to Emma as you work, and tell her what you're doing before you do it. That way she won't be nervous and she'll also have the chance to learn something."

Serena let out an aggravated sigh that sounded like she had something stuck in the back of her throat. "Fine," she said, sounding like me when I was being bratty on the phone with my mum earlier. I could feel a blush rising up my neck and into my cheeks.

"Emma," said Patricia. I glanced at her and found her smiling encouragingly once again. "Don't worry! You're going to do great! Just relax." She winked at me, and I felt better. "It's just makeup," she said, then she made a funny face at Serena's back, and I giggled.

"Right now I'm priming your eyelids," said Serena. "Close. It's a sponge with . . . uh . . . primer on it."

"And that's for . . ." prompted Patricia.

"That's to make sure all my hard work doesn't slide off under the lights," said Serena.

33

I could feel the sponge dabbing at my eyelids, and now that I knew what it was, it was actually kind of relaxing. There was a pause, and I opened my eyes again, but Serena quickly said, "Stay closed. Let it dry."

Next I felt a brush along my eyebrows. I raised them, and she said, "Hold still. I'm just darkening your brows a little. Brows are the first things to go in the lights. They just disappear."

I have pretty dark eyebrows, despite my blonde hair, so it was hard to imagine them disappearing at all (my mum won't let me tweeze them because, she says, they never grow back right).

Serena blew on my eyelids and it surprised me, but I did not open my eyes this time! I was learning!

"Okay, now I'm going to do a little base colour," she said. I felt a fluffy brush pouffing all over my eyelid. It felt nice. *I could get into this,* I thought. Once I knew not to be scared, it felt like I was being pampered.

"Now something darker in the crease," Serena continued, and there was more pouffing, but with what felt like a smaller brush.

"Open," she commanded. I did, and found her staring very hard at me, looking critically back and forth between my eyes. "A little more for the left," she said. "Close." And I closed, then there was pouffing, then, "Open."

Okay, maybe I couldn't get used to it. I was starting to feel a little bored.

"Liner," she said. "Or, actually, let me use a wet liner." She selected a long black tube from the box and unscrewed the cap, revealing a long wand with a tiny pointed paintbrush on the end. "You are going to need to hold very, very, *very* still. Because if you blink, and I mess up, we have to wipe all the eye makeup off and start over. Do you understand?" I nodded, nervous again.

Serena approached my eye with the wand, and I began to blink really fast. She stopped and looked at me carefully. "Can you hold still?" she asked, like she was trying really hard to be patient.

"Yes," I said. But as she started to approach my eye, I began to blink rapidly again.

"Okay." She put her hand down. "What am I supposed to do here?" she asked Patricia.

Patricia bit her lip, then she said, "Emma, honey, Serena is going to line your upper lid, from the inner corner to the outer corner, with some wet liner. It will not end up in your eye, but it might be a little cold and may be a tiny bit ticklish. You can stand it, though. Serena, why don't you stretch the lid out first, then approach it with your other hand. Emma, maybe just close your eyes."

I felt better now, knowing what to expect, and I closed my eyes and let Serena pull my eyelid one way, then the other way, out to the side. The liner *was* wet and tickly, but it wasn't too bad.

"Don't open. Not till I say so," ordered Serena.

She busied herself with her kit, and then after a minute or so (a long time to sit with your eyes closed in a room with other people, by the way), she said, "Open." And I did. I glanced in the mirror, and I couldn't believe what I saw. I looked like an adult! Or practically one. Like an old teenager.

"Wow!" I said, gaping at my reflection.

"I know," said Serena proudly.

"Hmm," said Patricia. "I think Mona is hoping for something a little more . . . wholesome. The dress she's thinking of is certainly more . . . innocent looking, maybe."

Serena looked at her, then back at me. "Just wait till you see it on the computer, okay? No changes till then." She rolled her eyes and muttered to herself; it sounded like, "Amateurs." Or maybe I just thought that was what she said because I had a guilty conscience about being inexperienced.

She withdrew a kind of scary-looking clamp from the kit and said, "Now we'll curl your eye-lashes."

"Umm . . . okaaay . . ." I said. Curly eyelashes? Who knew such a thing was desirable?

Serena had me close my eyes again, and then she clamped my lashes, each eye in turn, and she counted to thirty while she had them clamped.

When I opened my eyes and looked in the mirror again, my eyelashes didn't look curly, exactly, but their angle was definitely different. It made me look more awake or something, too. "Cool!" I said, turning my head from side to side to try to see my lashes at different angles.

"I think I'll skip the mascara," said Serena to herself. She selected a bottle of skin-coloured liquid and began to dab some around my face. "Just evening out your skin tone now," she said.

"Is it uneven?" I asked, my voice muffled as the sponge passed over my lips. Yuck!

"Everyone's is," said Serena, looking at me. "Shows up more in pictures. That's why we need to correct it first. Now some powder." There was lots of pouffing with the biggest brush yet. It felt great. "And some blush . . ."

Serena took another brush and dabbed from a

pink pot and onto my cheeks, nose, chin and fore-head.

"Hey! Blush is for your cheeks! I know that much!" I said.

Serena narrowed her eyes at me. "Not exclusively," she said.

Oh.

"It brightens up everything," offered Patricia, who'd been quietly watching.

"Some nude lip liner . . ." said Serena, outlining at my mouth with a kind of dry stick. That did *not* feel good.

I glanced in the mirror. Wow, did I look older!

Serena put her fingers under my chin and turned me back to face her again. She looked at me critically, leaning back, then leaning in. Squinting again.

"Oh, what the heck," she said, and she selected a dark tube of lipstick and dabbed it on my lips with a makeup brush. "There."

I looked in the mirror and couldn't believe it! I actually looked like a model! "Wow!" I said. If I hadn't known, I would have put my age at eighteen, at least. It was an incredible transformation.

Serena smiled like she was proud of herself. "I know. It's really an art."

I looked at Patricia. She didn't seem thrilled.

Her mouth was set in a kind of a line. "Let's see how Mona likes it," she said. "Come, Emma. Before we get the dress on, okay?"

"You might as well do the dress and give them the full effect . . ." said Serena. "It's kind of out of context like this, with the . . . jeans and whatnot." She gestured at my outfit in a dismissive way.

But Patricia ignored her. "Come," she said again.

We left the dressing room and went out into the main salon. Joachim and his team had finished setting up, and Mona and my dad were chatting in the seating area where I'd left him.

"Mona?" said Patricia, pushing me a little ahead of her into the room.

Mona and my dad turned and looked at me blankly. It was like they had no idea who I was for a minute. Then their faces changed.

My father came to his senses first. "No way!" he shouted as he jumped to his feet.

Mona stood quickly. "All wrong," she said emphatically.

And I burst into tears.

CHAPTER 4

Emma Taylor's a Hottie

Well, that was mortifying.

I had figured all along that my dad would embarrass me. I just didn't expect it would be in the form of a tirade against Serena, Joachim and the entire entertainment industry of America. The only good thing was that Mona was also mad, so it didn't look like my dad was a lone crazy person. She was yelling too.

It didn't take long for Serena to take off everything she had put on, even though I thought she wiped a little harder than she needed to. It wasn't my fault Mona had freaked out and my dad had wanted to pull me out right then and there. They said I looked *waaaay* too old and inappropriate and all sorts of other things I didn't really understand, but when they realised I was crying, they were quick to tell me it was totally not my fault, and everything began to settle down. That made me feel better.

Serena gave me some Visine for my eyes, and the redness went away pretty fast. After that, Mona stood by my side while Serena put a tiny bit of foundation on my skin, a trace of blush on my cheeks and a hint of pink on my lips, and that was it. Serena kept muttering about the computer and the lights, like before, but Mona was firm. "I'll take my chances," said Mona.

While I got on my dress, I could hear Mona through the door as she lectured Joachim and his team.

"I want this done quickly; I want the utmost care taken that the model is not taxed or upset; I want it clean, wholesome and pretty. And that's it. If any of it goes off track or gets too fresh or rude, you're fired and no one gets paid. Does everyone understand?" she said.

There was murmuring I couldn't hear, but I could tell that Mona had the last word.

After that, things *did* go quickly, and well. Patricia gave me a bouquet of white flowers to hold, and after a while they swapped it for a white basket tied with ribbons and filled with white rose

41

petals I had to scatter. They had me barefoot, with a crown of daisies – all sorts of looks. I didn't realise there were so many props available at The Special Day for junior bridesmaids!

I know I was pretty stiff at first. Joachim kept trying to tell me jokes to get me to relax. My dad got in on the act and started goofing around, and after a while we were all laughing, and it went by pretty fast. There was a lighting guy name Frank, and when the lights got too hot, he'd give me a little break in front of the fan, which was nice. And Stella, on the computer, let me see the shots she thought were the best. Right as I started to feel like I was dragging, Joachim said, "We've got it."

Patricia had me change and wash my face. I put my hair back in a ponytail, and I looked like my regular old self when it was time to leave. My dad made me go around and shake everyone's hand and thank him or her before we left. He thanked Mona, too, and they shared a laugh about the near disaster with my makeup. I felt funny listening to them, because I had thought I looked good in the makeup – like a real model, even if I did look much older. But the way they reacted was like I had looked ugly. I didn't really get it, but it made my face burn when I thought about it.

We were the first to leave. I could see Patricia had at least an hour to go of breaking down the equipment and then the cleanup, and I felt bad for her. I asked my dad if we could stay to help, but he said no. Mona overheard and said, "The talent never cleans up, darling! Run! You've worked hard all day!" She gave me an envelope with my pay, and I gave her and Patricia hugs good-bye; then my dad and I left.

It was dark when we drove out of the mall, and I couldn't believe I'd spent the whole day at work! Back home, my mum wanted to know every detail, but I felt like so much had happened, I didn't know where to begin. I told her a little, begged off, and then went upstairs to flop onto my bed. I'd meant to read or play my flute, but my eyes must've drifted shut. The next thing I knew, my mum was gently squeezing my shoulder, telling me it was dinner-time.

The following week flew by, and the next thing I knew, it was late Friday afternoon, and I was at Katie's, getting ready to deliver double-fudge cupcakes to a birthday party, followed by a trip to the movies with all the Cupcakers. As much as I had enjoyed working the weekend before, it was fun to just be a kid this weekend. I'd be back at The Special Day in the morning, but only for a few minutes, to drop off Mona's order. There weren't any trunk shows this weekend, and I was actually kind of glad about it.

Katie and I were in the kitchen packing the cupcakes into their carriers, Mia and Alexis had gone home to change, and suddenly Mrs Brown came into the kitchen. She was holding the local paper that comes out Fridays and kind of waving it around in the air.

"Emma, honey! Look! It's you!" she cried, her reading glasses slipping low on the bridge of her nose.

She spread out the back page of the first section onto the kitchen table, and there I was! A full-page ad of me, with my back to the camera, looking over my shoulder, and the flower bouquet in my hands and a closed-lipped smile on my face. The top of the ad read, JUNIOR BRIDESMAIDS BY JADEN SACKS, and the bottom had, THE SPECIAL DAY, CHAMBER STREET MALL.

"Oh! There I am! You're right!" I giggled. I was embarrassed to see myself there like that; I'd kind of forgotten that anyone could see the ad once it came out. I didn't know what to say. Plus, it was, like, a whole page. I mean, my face was huge!

Katie stood there staring at the photo, her mouth hanging open in shock. She looked up at me. "Emma! You're a model! For real!" she said, breathlessly.

I shrugged, still grinning like an idiot.

Mrs Brown gushed, "You look absolutely beautiful, honey. Simply gorgeous. I love it. I have to call your mum and tell her."

"But . . . I didn't realise . . . I mean, I know you said you'd be in the paper, but I kind of forgot. And here you are!" sputtered Katie, incredulous.

I laughed. "I didn't know when it would run, either. I just . . . I kind of forgot too!" I said. The truth was, I wasn't sure what to think about the whole photo shoot episode. Some of it was fun, some of it was funny, some of it was frustrating, and a lot of it was mortifying and upsetting, but Mona had given me one hundred and fifty dollars on top of my usual trunk-show payment! I hadn't really talked about any of it with Katie and the others, because I didn't know what to say. Now, I flipped over the paper to hide the photo. "Okay! Moving right along!" I said with a little laugh. (That's what my mum says to me sometimes when she wants to change the subject.) Katie was still looking at me oddly, like she wasn't sure who I was.

"Earth to Katie! Let's finish up these cupcakes so we can get to the cinema. Alexis will not be psyched if we're late."

Katie kind of came to, shaking her head as if to clear it. "So that's all? You just turn it over and move on?"

I punched Katie lightly on the arm and resumed my cupcake packing. "What do you want me to do? Drool all over the photo? Hug it? Cry? Come on, Katie!"

She laughed a little and then began helping me again with the cupcakes. "I don't know," she said finally. "I'm not sure what I'd do if I was you!"

At the movies, Mia and Alexis raced over when they saw us. "Emmaaaaa! We saw your photo! It's amaaaazing!" Mia said dramatically. She kept looking at me the way Katie had before, like she was searching for something in my face. Like she didn't really know me.

Only Alexis was totally normal. "I hope you got paid a lot for it," she said. "It's a totally huge ad, and the paper's circulation is about forty-five thousand. I googled it. So figure—"

"Stop!" I swatted her. "Look, it was a once-in-a-lifetime opportunity. I did it. It's over. It was kind of interesting, kind of hard. I did make some good money. And that's it. I'm just me. Just plain Emma." I smiled and shrugged at them. "Same old, same old."

"Emma!" cried someone behind me. We all turned to look. It was Olivia Allen. Ugh!

Olivia is a girl in our class, and none of us like her. She's new, and she kind of used Mia when she first moved here; then she dropped her like a hot potato for the superpopular girls in the Best Friends Club. They're basically our enemies, which means we were *not* psyched to see Olivia and two of her henchmen, Bella and Maggie, here tonight.

"Emma!" She got closer. "OMG! We saw your *photo*! In the *paper*! We didn't know you were *modelling*!" she shrieked.

Well, it's not like we're friends, so how would you know anything I'm up to? I wanted to ask. But instead I shrugged. "Yeah, I guess so," I said, looking around uneasily, to make sure no one else had heard. "Just a little."

Olivia came over and then looped her arm through mine and kind of pulled me away from my friends and towards hers. "Tell me everything. Do you have an agent? How many go-sees are you doing each week? What's your portfolio like? Online or hard copies?"

I was overwhelmed. Why was she suddenly being so chummy? Was it just because of my ad? And how did she know so much about modelling?

"Actually," I said, removing my arm from hers. "I do trunk shows at The Special Day bridal salon, and they just asked if I'd do this one ad for them. So I said yes. That's all it was." I looked at the Cupcakers, who were all watching me solemnly as I spoke with the enemy.

"Oh!" Olivia looked disappointed. Bella and Maggie looked bored. "Well, if you ever want to talk shop, just let me know," said Olivia. "I've had lots of experience in that world." She rolled her eyes, like it tired her out just thinking about all the experience she'd had. I knew that was my cue to ask her what she knew and how she knew it, but I just couldn't bring myself to start a bragathon with her.

"Okay," I said. "I will. Um. Thanks. Enjoy the movie!" And I turned my back on Olivia and then grabbed my friends, walking us to the concession stand.

"What was *that* all about?" I muttered as soon as we were out of earshot. "Is Olivia Allen a model?"

"I think she might have been in an ad when she was younger," said Mia.

We walked past a couple of girls from the grade below us at school. I smiled, and one of them whispered to the other, "That's her!"

"Hi, Emma!" they cried in unison, then they turned away, blushing and giggling.

"I guess a lot of people read the *Gazette*!" said Katie, impressed.

"Maybe we should run an ad for the Cupcake Club!" said Alexis.

I laughed. Two girls – except this time from the grade above us – said hi to me while we were buying our popcorn, and then a bunch more girls said hi to me when we got into the cinema.

"I'm telling you, Emma. You're the new Romaine Ford," said Alexis.

"I feel like we're out with a celebrity!" Katie squealed.

I swatted her. "Stop!" But it was kind of true. I did feel . . . special. It was fun being recognised and spoken to. Even the attention from Olivia was kind of pleasant. *This must be what it feels like to be famous,* I thought as the lights dimmed and the pre-show silence-your-mobile-phone announcements started.

Suddenly, a boy's voice rang out of the dark. "Emma Taylor's a hottie!" and a bunch of people laughed.

My face instantly grew hot as I squirmed in my seat. I felt people looking at me, but I kept my eyes on the screen, like I hadn't heard.

Alexis, who was sitting next to me, reached for my hand and squeezed it. She seemed to be saying, *Don't worry* and *Isn't this exciting?* all at once. I squeezed back, saying, *Yes*, *No* and *Thanks*.

CHAPTER 5

Bambini di Roma

On Saturday afternoon I came home from orchestra practice and found my mum in the kitchen paying the bills.

"Hi, Emma!" she said brightly. "How was it?"

I got an apple and told her all about practice and our pieces and the new assistant conductor. She grilled me about what I still had for homework (everything), and I had to tell her my plan for getting it all done.

Finally, she put her palms flat on the table and took a deep breath. Looking down at the table, she said, "Sweetheart, Mona called with an opportunity for you. She said the head of publicity at Miller's called her for your contact info. They'd seen the beautiful ad in the *Gazette* yesterday, and they want to ask you to do some modelling for them, in-store and maybe in print." She looked up at me. "She wanted to know if she should give them our number."

I took a bite of my apple and then chewed. I thought about the photo session and mean Serena, and my dad embarrassing me. But then I thought about the money and all the nice feedback at the cinema. Miller's department store was big and really chic. They had cool ads, and not just in the *Gazette*, but in big local magazines, and sometimes billboards, too.

"Yes," I replied, not meeting her eye.

"Emma," said my mum.

I looked up.

"Do you really want to do this?" she asked.

"Yes," I said again.

She sighed. "What do you like about it?" she asked.

"Um, the money. The . . . attention," I added, feeling shy saying it.

"Don't we give you enough attention? Are you feeling neglected, sweetheart? Oh, I knew it! I just knew——"

"Mum! Stop! It's not about you guys. It's about me! It's fun being recognised. It's fun being fussed over. It's fun being all girlie for a day, okay? And they pay me for all that! What's not to like?" Besides mean makeup artists and unpredictable popular girls and people shouting at the cinema, even if they are saying nice things – for now. But I didn't say any of that.

Mum nodded, thinking. "Well, I can see the appeal when you put it that way. Your dad and I will need to discuss it, and we'll have to set some guidelines. Like, local work only. That will probably be one. And only on weekends. And one of us will always go with you. Hmm . . . I think I'd better go online and do a little research on how to be the mother of a model!"

She reached over and gave my hand a squeeze. "I'm sorry if I sounded negative. It *is* exciting, sweetheart," she whispered.

I smiled. "I know," I said.

"And we're proud of you."

"Thanks."

Just then my brother Matt walked in, bursting the bubble.

"Dude. Everyone's talking about your picture," he said, opening the cabinet and taking out a glass with a clatter. He poured himself a tall drink of milk.

53

"Oh yeah?" I asked casually, then added, "I hope they're saying nice things?" I wasn't exactly fishing for compliments, but I wouldn't have minded if he wanted to pass any along.

"Yeah. Josh Samuels thinks you're totally hot. He's carrying the page from the paper around in his knapsack. And Brewer Jones said you looked hot too."

"Oh." Josh and Brewer aren't exactly the coolest guys in the world. And they're not particularly cute either. They're just normal.

"What about Joe Fraser?" I asked. "Has he said anything?"

Matt chugged his milk. After he finished, he wiped his milk mustache with the back of his hand and then let out a huge burp.

"Matthew!" scolded my mother.

Matt grinned. "Nope. Joey hasn't said a word. Want me to tell him you were asking what he thought of it?"

"Matt, if you dare . . ." I leaped out of my seat and lunged at him.

"Children!" said my mother sternly. "That's enough."

Matt cackled and dodged out of the way. "I'll tell him you're framing a copy of the ad for him for

54

his birthday, and you're signing it 'Love and kisses, Emmy'!" Matt dropped his glass in the sink and scooted out the door.

"Mum!" I protested.

"Emma." She sighed wearily. "This is something I cannot control. You remember me mentioning that just this sort of thing might happen. Makes you think twice, doesn't it?" She looked at me knowingly.

"Oh, whatever," I said. I folded my arms across my chest and looked away.

"I know, but it's hard to have your cake and eat it too," said my mum with raised eyebrows.

I hate know-it-alls.

That night my mum and my dad and I had a meeting. We listed the pros (good money, nice feedback, work experience) and the cons (hard work, overexposure, lots of strong personalities to deal with) of modelling and talked about the guidelines my mum had mentioned earlier.

My parents really were reluctant to let me expand beyond The Special Day. But I reasoned that the extra money would be handy, and I promised I would put at least half of it in my university fund. I pointed out that work experience is always important and that I'd be learning to get along with all types of personalities. Plus, they'd be there on the shoots with me! Finally, I think I just wore them down with my begging because they looked at each other, and my dad shrugged.

"Fine, we give in!" he said. "Right, Wendy?"

"Yes. But as your managers," she continued, grinning, "we reserve the right to turn down jobs and to take you out of any jobs we feel are not appropriate. Understood?"

"Yes! Oh, Mum, thanks! And Dad! Thanks, you guys, you won't regret it!" I hugged them both and then ran upstairs to let my friends know that I was officially a model.

My first job for Miller's was two Saturdays later, after lunch. They had in a new line of children's wear from Europe, and they hired four models to walk all around the store wearing it and carrying a little sign saying, BAMBINI DI ROMA, 4TH FLOOR. The other kids were younger than me, so they were allowed to walk together, but the publicity person wanted me out there on my own. I hated to say it, but it was kind of lonely and boring. Plus, the clothes were majorly babyish if you ask me.

My first look was a red smocked dress with a

white Peter Pan collar. I don't know how kids in Rome dress, but if they're still made to wear this stuff after they turned ten, I would think there'd be a mutiny. They put my hair back with a thick, black, velvet headband, which I also didn't like, but at least I didn't have to wear any makeup. The people working with me were nice but very professional. They barely remembered my name, and they certainly didn't chat with me the way Patricia always does. It was okay, though. No one was mean or anything. It was just work. They were professionals, and they just assumed I was too. Which I was!

They gave me my sign to carry, and I left my mum upstairs and then took the elevator down to the ground floor to walk around. I knew how to do this: Make eye contact, smile, hold up the sign a little and twirl. It wasn't hard.

Only it was hard.

No one really looked at me.

I smiled harder and twirled more often, but I began to feel like I was invisible. My mum was still upstairs in the lounge, doing some needlepoint and waiting for me. I felt I could leave and no one would notice. At one point I crossed paths with the other models, in their little threesome. They were being shepherded by the publicity lady, and people were fawning all over them, like, "Oh, aren't they cute?" and "Isn't this outfit darling?" It made me cranky just watching, but I am, after all, a professional now, so I smiled and waved and twirled myself right on to another floor.

I realised my mistake only a second too late.

"Emma!" a voice squealed.

I was in the teen department.

I spun around, face-to-face with none other than Olivia Allen.

"Hey!" I said, trying to drum up some enthusiasm.

"Hey yourself!" cried Olivia, kind of swatting my arm (a little hard, if you ask me). "You said you only model for that bridal place!" She narrowed her eyes, but smiling like she was being friendly.

"Yeah, well . . . Miller's made me an offer I couldn't refuse," I said, joking.

"*Really,*" said Olivia, more as a statement than a question. Oops. I guess she believed me. Whatever.

Bella, Maggie and Callie joined her side. *Do these girls ever do anything alone?* I wondered. "Hi," I said weakly. They were dressed to the nines in all sorts of chic ensembles. (Why are they clothes shopping if they look this good already?) I was suddenly aware of my childish outfit, so I started edging away before anyone could say anything.

"Okay, so . . ." I mumbled.

"Wow, isn't runway work just draining?" asked Olivia, all concerned. She looked at her friends, and they all nodded sympathetically, like they did it all the time and were exhausted just thinking about it.

"Well, I don't know that this is really *runway* work," I said. But Olivia wasn't actually interested in what I had to say. Although she posed her statements as questions, all she really wanted to do was share her own experiences. She continued.

"Well, your feet will be just killing you at the end of the day." Olivia glanced down at the ruffled white ankle socks and black patent leather Mary Janes the publicity people wedged me into. Her nose wrinkled in distaste. "When you do TV work, there are lots of breaks in the trailer, and they have all kinds of snacks laid out at the craft services table. Yummy bagels and cookies and all sorts of treats. And they'll bring you anything you want if they don't have it there, you know. You just ask, and your wish is their command."

"Wow," said Bella appreciatively.

Olivia continued to nod dreamily.

I wanted to burst her bubble by asking her

exactly what kind of work she'd done to earn being treated like Angelina Jolie on set, but I didn't think it would be appropriate for a shop employee to be rude to a customer. Also, I didn't want to prolong the conversation and end up getting caught chatting on the job.

"Well, I need to go. It's time for my next look," I said, glancing at my wrist where my watch usually lives. (They made me take it off upstairs because it didn't go with the outfit. Probably because the six-year-olds who'd usually be wearing this outfit can't tell the time!)

"Of course. You're working. We shouldn't interrupt at all. I, of all people, understand," said Olivia solemnly.

"Right. Thanks, um . . . bye," I said.

But of course as I tried to edge away inconspicuously, two grannies accosted me and trapped me there for five full minutes, feeling the material of my dress and asking all about Bambini di Roma. I tried not to look at Olivia and her group, but they hadn't budged. The other three stood rapt while Olivia apparently imparted all her knowledge about the wide world of modelling.

As I finally left for good, Olivia called out, "Bye, Emma! Have fun! Talk soon!"

I was confused. Olivia was being totally nice, so why didn't I trust her?

The afternoon went slowly as I worked my way through eight Bambini di Roma outfits. My mum smiled supportively whenever I came back for an outfit change. She fed me some snacks and brushed my hair and gave me a hug each time. I wished I could stay with her. Or better yet, drag her to the teen department to shop with me. But we didn't have time. By the time I finished at five o'clock, we needed to get home, so she could cook dinner, and then we had to run over to see my oldest brother Sam's basketball game.

At the end, the publicity lady handed me an envelope with a check for two hundred and fifty dollars! I couldn't believe it. I smiled and shook her hand, like my dad had told me to, and said good-bye.

The lady paused, and then in a low voice she said to me and my mum, "I don't usually do this, but you are such a dear to work with and just so lovely looking. My very good friend is a big modelling agent in the city, and she asks me to keep an eye out only for exceptional talent to refer to her." She reached in to her desk drawer and pulled out a shiny gold business card that she handed to my mum. "Why

61

don't you give her a call if you aren't already working with an agent. She's tough, but she's the best in the business. I'll tell her to look out for your call. Thanks again, Emma. It was so nice meeting you, and we will certainly be in touch with more work for you very soon."

"Thank you. It was a nice opportunity. And thanks for the card," I said.

In the lift I leaned against my mum and read the card.

Alana Swenson

Representation

(913) 555-3798

"Huh. We'll have to Google her," I said, clueless.

CHAPTER 6

The Big Time

*T*yler Jones, Randi MacNeil, Josanna *and* Mallory Cordite! *All of them!*" I cried incredulously. I was reading from the Internet to my mum as she made dinner. I'd searched Alana Swenson as soon as we got home, only to find out she was basically the biggest modelling agent in New York, representing every major model I'd ever heard of. "Wow!"

"That *is* amazing," agreed my mum, then added, smiling, "*I've* even heard of some of them."

I sat, also smiling, and shaking my head in disbelief. The Swenson Group's home page was just a phone number. I guess that's all she needed.

The phone rang, and I saw on the caller ID that it was Alexis.

"Hey! How did it go?" she asked.

"Good! Actually, bad. It was really boring, but I did a good job, I guess."

"Of course you did!" said Alexis. "What else is up?"

"Well, they gave me a business card for an agent. I'm trying to convince my mum to call her," I said, glaring meaningfully at my mother.

"Not till I speak with your father!" she sing-songed for the tenth time.

I made a sound of aggravation. "What are you up to?" I asked Alexis.

"Not much. Homework. Just calling to make sure you're coming over to bake tomorrow. We've got that baby shower in the afternoon for Mrs Kramer's daughter."

"Right! I almost forgot. Yes, I will totally be there," I said, smacking my forehead. I mentally reviewed the mounds of homework I had upstairs. "What time?"

"Eleven, okay?" she asked.

"Yup. Sure. No prob. See you then."

We hung up, and I groaned.

"What?" asked my mum.

"Work, work, work," I said.

My mum said nothing. Right. Be careful what you wish for.

"I can't go to Sam's game," I said.

"Oh, honey! That's too bad. It's the semifinals!"

I shrugged. "Homework. I need to get it done tonight, so I can go bake tomorrow. Sorry."

"You don't have to apologise to me. It's Sam who will miss you."

"I'm sure!" I snorted. "Not a game goes by where Sam doesn't seek me out in the crowd."

"Well, I'll miss you, then," my mum said, knowing that to contradict me on this was pointless since I was right. Though we do try to make it to everyone's games when we can, with the amount of sports that go on in this family, there are a lot of missed games too. It's okay. Sam really wouldn't mind.

As I closed my laptop to go upstairs, the phone rang. My mum peeked at the caller ID and said, "It's for you, sweetheart."

SPECIAL DAY, THE, it said.

"Hello?" I answered.

"Darling, I have the most divine news!" It was Mona.

I smiled. "What?"

"Jaden Sacks has given us her line to carry – permanently. It's just incredibly exciting! We're all pinching ourselves!"

"Congratulations, Mona! That's great news!" I said. I was really happy for her. She'd worked so hard for this.

"I know. I'm thrilled. Anyway, we're going to have a launch party and runway show here at the store, one month from today, and I wanted to make sure my top model wasn't booked. I think Ms Sacks herself will be coming! Oh, it's just too exciting to think about!"

"Sure! I can be there, no problem. I'll double-check with my mum, but I'm sure it's okay." I noticed my mother looking at me. "Thanks for asking me!"

"Also, darling, it will be quite a crowd, and there probably will be some press, so let's go ahead and amp up the cupcake order. Maybe do something over the top, okay?"

"Great! We'd love to!" I couldn't wait to tell Alexis. A big cupcake order, and press!

"Okay, darling. Now that I'm in your book, I feel much better. Have a fabulous night. Kiss, kiss. Talk soon."

"Bye!" I said, and hung up.

"What's up?" asked my mum.

"Mona got the Jaden Sacks account! She's going to carry the line for good!"

"Great!" said my mum. "And more work for you?"

I nodded happily. "I'm going to model at the launch, a month from today, and Mona wants a big splashy cupcake order for the party."

"That's wonderful, dear. I'm so happy for you."

I hugged myself a little, feeling great, and picked my laptop back up. "I've got to let the others know."

"Okay, I'll call you for dinner in a little while."

Upstairs, I shot out a quick e-mail to the group to let them know about our new job. Alexis replied instantly, saying we'd brainstorm during our baking session at Mia's tomorrow, and I got to work on my homework. There was quite a lot of it.

At Mia's the next day, we were all buzzing with ideas for the Jaden Sacks launch party. Alexis suggested minis with Jaden Sacks's logo (it's an intertwined *J* and *S* inside a heart) on them, which I thought was cute but might be hard to execute. Mia suggested we create a stencil in the shape of the logo and just sift pale blue sugar through it onto each cupcake, and we agreed that would be really cool. But it was Katie who reminded us of our early days and of one of our ideas for Mia's mum's wedding, which had been to do a cupcake tower with tiers, so it looked like a wedding cake. And that was it, we were sold.

As the Kramers' cupcakes baked, Mia sketched a design on a piece of paper, and we all crowded around her, offering ideas and details. Katie thought fresh flowers would look pretty – maybe with some ivy hanging down – and we agreed, but Alexis cautioned us about cost, reminding us we didn't want to lose money on this project. In the end we were set on a plan, and Alexis promised to cost it out and get Mona's sign-off on it.

"Girls! Yoo-hoo!" Mrs Valdes was home.

"In here, Mum!" called Mia.

"Oh, I'm so happy you're all here, *mis amores*! I have some great news!" Mrs Valdes was beaming, her dark hair piled atop her head in a gorgeous bun, and a fitted dark-gray jumper and black leggings completing her casual-chic weekend look. She was such a glamorous mum.

Mia looked up, and her mum reached to wipe a trace of icing sugar off her cheek.

"I just ran into an old magazine colleague of mine, and we had a long chat. She was filling me in on what she does these days, and guess what? She's a food stylist and photographer. She's just starting up her own studio in the city, so she offered to take some photos of your cupcake creations for free if she could use them for publicity!" Mrs Valdes clapped her hands happily and did a little dance in place, tossing her head from side to side.

"Awesome!" I cried, and all us Cupcakers hooted and high-fived.

"Now, maybe we can do a website!" said Alexis. "I've been pricing it out for a while, and this could be just the thing that makes the numbers work – free publicity photos!"

"When would we do the shoot?" asked Katie.

"Whenever you like, but the sooner the better. And weekends are fine!" said Mrs Valdes.

"Cool! Thanks, Mami!" Mia gave her mum a big hug. "Our cupcakes are going to be models! Just like Emma!"

We all laughed.

"So what should we make for the portfolio?" asked Katie eagerly.

Mrs Valdes laughed, then said, "I'll leave you to the important part. Just let me know what day you'd like for me to set it up." And off she went to make herself an espresso at the fancy machine on the counter.

We began brainstorming, with me taking notes.

Alexis decided we needed to make ten examples of our "greatest hits," and we started to list them. Among them we had clown cupcakes that we did for little kids' birthdays (with an upside-down ice-cream cone as a clown hat on top); Jake Cakes ("dirt with worms" cupcakes, like we made for my brother Jake's birthday); caramel cupcakes with bacon frosting (my invention); minis, like we make for Mona; little "gift" cupcakes, like we made for Alexis's sister Dylan's sweet sixteen; the tiered wedding cake idea; Millionaires, which had expensive ingredients; and more. We started to realise it would be a lot to coordinate, and some of the cupcakes would be hard to transport (like the tiered wedding cake), so maybe we wouldn't do them all. But as Mia pointed out, a lot of them we could assemble at the studio, so it was really only a matter of bringing in the supplies. We narrowed it down to ten and then voted to confirm it.

This was going to be so much fun! We ordered pizza and then spent the day finishing the Kramers' cupcakes and refining our plan for the shoot. Of course, Alexis wasn't wild about spending a lot of money on supplies for cupcakes we wouldn't be selling, but we pointed out that business development is priceless, and she relented.

❀

It was late afternoon by the time we'd finished with the Kramers and everything, and I headed home for Sunday dinner. I found my parents at the kitchen table, peeling potatoes and the timing was perfect for us to discuss Alana Swenson. My mum had already filled in my dad, so all I had to do was beg.

"Please, Dad! Don't you see what a great opportunity this would be?"

My dad sighed. "I guess I'm unsure of your motivations. Is it the money? Are you interested in fame? Do you enjoy the process? Is it more fun than the other stuff you do and so you don't mind making sacrifices? It would be easier for me if I understood where you're coming from," he said.

I had to stop and think about all that for a minute. He raised some good points. After a moment I said, "All of it, I guess. I love making money. It's fun to be all girlie and get dressed up and be around pretty clothes and stuff. It's exciting to have people see your picture in the paper, and it would be neat to have some more of that. I don't know about fame. That seems like a lot of work. But I'd like to be recognised, anyway, as a model. That would be cool." It felt weird saying it – like, kind of embarrassing – but it was true. I looked

71

over my shoulder to make sure Matt hadn't snuck up behind me to eavesdrop and then torture me with my confession later. But the coast was clear, thank goodness.

"And the sacrifices?" my dad prompted.

I shrugged. "I already make a lot of sacrifices for work. I'm used to it," I said. "Dog walking, Cupcake Club, babysitting, The Special Day . . ."

My dad and mum looked at each other, and both seemed to be thinking.

Finally, my mum said, "Well, I guess we should at least give it a try. Emma, you certainly have a great work ethic, and I'd like to encourage that. Let's see what this Alana Swenson says, and we'll take it from there. But here are the ground rules: A parent will always go with you. The work has to be age appropriate. You will put ninety percent of your earned money into savings, and you can keep ten percent to spend." My mum was ticking things off on her potato-peely fingers. She looked at my dad. "What am I forgetting?"

"Good grades," he offered.

"Right. Your grades must stay above a B plus average, or we take a break from the modelling. And that's not just because we're worried about it eating into your study time, though we are. It's because

72

your schoolwork and brain development matter more than your looks, and they always will. That is our priority in this family. And no big egos, okay?"

I was so excited, I would have agreed to anything. I jumped up and hugged them both. "Great! Thanks, Mum. Thanks, Dad! I can't wait! Can I go tell my friends?"

My dad laughed. "Sure. They can say they knew you when . . ."

But my mum said, "Honey, I don't mean to be a killjoy, but let's not get too far ahead of ourselves. We haven't even spoken with this Swenson person yet . . ."

The next day my mum spoke to Ms Swenson while I was at school, and it went well. She relayed the conversation to me when I got home, and I guess it was a pretty short one. Ms Swenson said her friend from the shop had called her to tell her she'd given us the business card and to look out for us since I was "beautiful" and "very natural" (!!!!). Ms Swenson told my mum to e-mail her five casual, nonprofessional photos of me with no makeup or hair styling, in certain poses. But she said that this was just a formality: If her scout thought I was a fit, then I probably was. We'd meet as soon as possible and get things rolling (her words). And that was the whole conversation!

Needless to say, I wanted to take the photos and e-mail them in immediately, but my mum said since my dad was a great photographer, we'd have him come home early from work the next day and take the photos in the garden. Also needless to say, when I told the Cupcakers this news, they all insisted on coming over for the shoot, and Mia said she'd have her mum put a few looks together for her to bring to me before she went to a meeting in the city.

At lunch the next day, Mia, Katie, Alexis and I were sitting together (of course), discussing the outfits Mia had packed for me, when Olivia Allen came walking by with her crew.

"Hey, Emma, how's the modelling going?" she asked, all interested and cool. She waved breezily at Mia and ignored Katie and Alexis, as usual. Mia had been Olivia's first friend when she moved to Maple Grove, but Olivia had dumped her in favour of the more trendy popular girls, Callie, Maggie and Bella. Now she acted kind of friendly to Mia but never called her or invited her to anything. Mia didn't care anymore, but it made me mad on her behalf.

"Oh, it's going . . ." I said, letting my words just trail off vaguely. I didn't want to let her in on any more information, but unfortunately Katie didn't get my hint.

"Emma has an agent! A famous one!" said Katie.

I glared at her for blabbing, but she didn't notice.

Olivia's eyes widened, and she turned back to look at me a little more carefully this time. "Well, my goodness, that's exciting!" she said, sounding like a grown-up. "I doubt I would have ever heard of any of the agents around here, but try me. Who is it?" She arranged her face into kind of a bored expression.

Now I was annoyed, and this made me competitive. I couldn't wait for her reaction. "Alana Swenson," I said, all casual.

Olivia's eyes nearly popped out of her head. Her face turned bright red. "Did you say Alana Swenson? Are you *kidding* me? She's the top agent in the world! I am *freaking out* right now!"

And she did look like she was freaking out.

Olivia spluttered, "I need to go call my mum! I mean, I . . . I nearly signed with Alana a couple of years ago, but then . . . well, my mum thought I was getting overexposed or something . . ." She blushed and looked away.

Right.

"Do you have her number?" she pressed.

"It's at home," I said, shrugging.

"Oh, right. Wow. Okay. Uh ... I've gotta go. Talk to you very, *very* soon," she said. And she was off, with her gang tagging along.

"I can't wait," I said to her back as she disappeared from sight.

"Typical Olivia Allen, hot and cold," said Alexis. "One day she's your best friend; the next day you're dead to her. She likes to keep 'em guessing."

"Trust me, I'm not guessing!" I said, and we all laughed.

"You know the only modelling she's ever done was a baby food advert when she was, like, one year old," said Mia quietly.

"Whaaaat?" I couldn't believe that! "Are you sure?"

Mia nodded. "I mean, I guess she might have been trying off and on since then to get more work, but that's the only actual job she's ever had. She sent me the link on YouTube."

"Oh, we have *got* to see that!" said Alexis. "Priceless."

"Wait, but if the commercial is, like, twelve years old, then how come it's on YouTube?" asked

Katie. "YouTube wasn't even invented then!"

Mia rolled her eyes. "Olivia put it up, of course!" she said.

"Oh boy." I was embarrassed for Olivia now. "Shoot me if I ever get that cuckoo about modelling, okay? Promise!"

"We will, don't worry! If you get too big for your britches, well . . . just watch out!" Alexis wagged her finger at me.

I laughed. "I knew I could count on you." But inside I felt a little pang. I wish I could have them around during the jobs. Modelling was kind of lonely. Oh well. At least the money was good.

CHAPTER 7

Alana Swenson

After school the girls came to my house, we all had a snack, and then Mia dressed me up. The outfits were cute, with Mrs Valdes's signature touches — great scarves in gorgeous colours, a fun slouchy hat to crush on my head, cool earrings — and other than that, totally age appropriate (as my mum would say) clothes that I would normally wear. I was psyched. The looks were great, and Mrs Valdes and Mia had organised each outfit with coordinating accessories zipped into a Ziploc bag and taped to the hanger. It couldn't have been easier to get dressed!

My dad came home as I was ready in my first look and my mother was fighting off Mia, who had a tube of dark lipstick in her hand.

"She said no makeup!" my mother protested,

laughing as she tried to grab the lipstick from Mia's hand.

"Please, Mrs Taylor! A strong lip would just complete the whole look!" Mia giggled, dodging out of my mum's reach.

"A strong lip!" My dad laughed incredulously as he walked into the room. "That sounds like something you'd get from an enemy in the playground!"

"Oh, Dad!" I said. "You're hopeless!"

"Let's get this show on the road!" my dad instructed, hoisting his camera.

Mia gave up on the lipstick, and we tumbled out into the garden where my mum had hung a white flat sheet over the back fence. The light was pretty good, according to my dad, since the sun was kind of low in the sky. He took a bunch of photos of me in the first outfit, with the Cupcakers all oohing and aahing as I went through the poses Alana Swenson had asked for: three-quarter turn, head-on, looking up, head shot and full body. My mum would later send her my measurements.

We worked our way through the three outfits Mia had put together, and I tried to be patient with my dad, pretending he was a professional, just like Joachim, but it was not easy. Just as we were finishing the third outfit, the phone rang, and my mum went inside to answer it.

"Honey, it's someone called Olivia Allen? I told her you were in the middle of something, and she said she just needs a phone number from you?" my mum called from the back door.

The Cupcakers and I all looked at one another in shock.

"OMG!" I said. "The nerve!"

Alexis was shaking her head.

"Pushy, pushy," said Katie.

"What are you going to do?" asked Mia.

I thought for a second. "Just tell her to Google it. It'll come up," I called back to my mum.

My mum gave me the thumbs-up, but was back in a flash. "She wants to know if she can use your name."

Now my jaw dropped at the nerve. "NO!" I yelled so emphatically that my mum raised her palms in the air, like, *Sorry, I'm just the messenger.*

"Wow!" I said to my friends, shaking my head.

"Over here, Emma! Stay focused!" called my dad, then muttered, "I can't believe I actually just said that."

"Yes, *focus*, Emma, for goodness' sake!" said Alexis, all fake businesslike. She made a funny face at me, and seeing her, so did Katie. Pretty soon my friends were all hamming it up, and my dad told them if they were going to work so hard, they should be in the photos too.

"Hey! A group shot for our website!" said Alexis.

Mia laughed. "Of course. All for business!"

"Well, you never know," said Alexis as my dad snapped away, the four of us in different silly, cute and serious poses. It was really fun, and I have to say I liked it better when I wasn't the only one in the frame.

Later, after everyone had left, I got an IM from Olivia. It said,

Swenson wants me too! Yay! Modelling buddies!

I wanted to throw up.

Two days later I was sitting in Alana Swenson's waiting area with my mum after having taken the train into the city after school. I couldn't believe how fast things were moving, but I was pretty psyched. I hadn't seen Olivia at school since she'd told me she was also signing with Alana Swenson, so I planned on mentioning her to Alana to see what she said. I had a sneaky feeling what Olivia had said wasn't true, but I couldn't be sure.

My parents and I had selected five photos the night my dad had taken them, and my mum had e-mailed them. We heard back from Alana that very night. She replied to my mum's e-mail, asking her to call her assistant in the morning to book an appointment. I think my parents were kind of rattled by the speed of the whole thing too, but they were trying to act like they were in control.

Alana Swenson's waiting area was windowless, stark, and modern – all black and grey rugs and upholstery, and very hushed, except for the phones, which purred and buzzed nonstop. There were six beautiful young women at a long counterlike desk, answering the phones. The women were all different ethnicities, like a United Nations of model wannabes, and they all wore headsets and spoke so quietly into them that I couldn't hear a thing they were saying.

We were the only visitors.

Exactly thirty seconds after our appointment time, a door opened and another beautiful young woman silently beckoned us with a curved finger. We stood and followed her down a quiet hall, dim and spare, passing closed doors on either side until reaching the final closed door at the very end of the hall. The woman tapped on the door and opened it, and I had to wince at the instant brightness.

There were wraparound windows and gold everywhere – gold desk, gold-tiled floor, golden lamps, gold painted walls – the whole room glowed gold.

And sitting at the desk in a gold swivel chair was a tiny woman with golden hair pulled back into a tight bun, and gold-framed glasses on her tiny nose. She was the size of a child!

"Hello, Taylors! I am Alana Swenson!" Despite her size, she had the raspy, booming voice of a very large person. I was totally caught off guard. I wanted to laugh, but managed it down to just a big grin.

"I know, I know, none of this was what you expected!" she boomed. "That's the point! Have a seat! You are lovely looking! Trina was right. I'm glad she sent you. This won't take long."

My mum and I sat in two additional gold swivel chairs in front of the desk, and Alana proceeded to hand us paperwork (agent contracts, agency rules, this week's list of open calls, my website's username and password) and briefly explain it all. There will be go-sees, where I am invited to try out for a job. I will be told what to wear and where to go. The client will let Alana know if I get the job. My money will be sent to Alana, who will take twenty percent and send me a check for the rest. Alana was talking very quickly, and my mother was nodding and writing everything down in her notebook.

"All right! Any questions?" Alana asked.

I didn't have any. "It all sounds great!" I said, hoping to appear perky.

"It's hard work," Alana pointed out.

Right.

"What about school?" asked my mother.

Alana shrugged. "With looks like hers, this one will make more money than any education could give her." Alana laughed – "Heh, heh, heh" – like she was drowning.

My mum's jaw dropped, but then she recovered. "I meant, the go-sees are after school and on weekends, right?"

Alana's phone buzzed. She put her hand to the receiver to answer. "Not always. Any other questions?"

My mother and I looked at each other. I shook my head.

"Uh . . ." said my mother.

"Alana Swenson," said Alana, picking up her phone, she waved and mouthed *Bye* at us.

We stood up and found our escort back at the door to take us out.

"Thank you," I said over my shoulder. Alana waved again.

Moments later we were out on the street, and my mother and I looked at each other and then burst out laughing.

"Was that for real?" I asked her.

"No, I think it was a scene from a movie!" she said.

"OMG." We stood for a minute and caught our breath. I couldn't stop thinking about what Alana had said about school. "Mum?" I began.

"No. I know what you're thinking. Listen, sweetheart, you're certainly beautiful, but no one is that beautiful. School comes first, and it always will. Look, you don't even know if you like modelling yet. Let's take things one step at a time."

"Fine," I said. And I have to admit, I was a little relieved.

It wasn't until the train ride home that I realised I'd never had a chance to ask Alana if it was true about Olivia. Oh well. I'd find out sooner or later.

sparkle

CHAPTER 8

Modelling Buddies

The next couple of days I rushed home from school to see if I'd received any assignments from Alana, but there was nothing. My mum said to be patient and that it was better to ease into things, but I just wanted to get started.

It wasn't until Friday that I finally ran into Olivia in the cafeteria. She looked caught, like a deer in headlights, when I spied her.

"Hi, Olivia," I said. I couldn't wait to get to the bottom of her Alana story.

"Oh, hi, Emma, I'm just running out . . . I'm late for a meeting with my lab partner . . ." She scrambled a little, trying to get away from me, but I wasn't going to let her get off that easily.

"So what's up with Alana Swenson? I've

been meaning to ask you, but I haven't seen you around."

"Oh, you know." Olivia shrugged. "She was supernice. She said to send in my photos and she'd take a look, so . . ."

Olivia was acting like she was still waiting to hear back, but I knew how quickly Alana responded to things. Olivia must've been rejected. "So what did she say?" I pressed. I didn't want to be mean, but I also was annoyed at Olivia for lying and trying to kind of steal my thunder.

"Well . . . they're pretty busy right now, so, you know . . ."

"It didn't work out?" I asked flat out.

"No, she said to check back, though, maybe when I grow a little."

Bingo! Rejected! Just as I suspected.

"Oh, okay. Well, keep me posted, anyway," I said, "and good luck!"

I am not a mean person, but I hate liars, and it felt good to call Olivia out on her lie. That said, I did feel a little sorry for her. Being rejected stinks, and when it's for something as personal as your looks, well, it has got to be hard.

"Yeah, I think I'm hitting some open calls this weekend, if you're interested. I'll have my mum call your mum, okay?" And she took off before I could say not to bother.

I sighed. Oh whatever.

When I got home after baking minis for Mona at Katie's all afternoon, my mum was already back from work and all a-chatter about the great conversation she'd had on the phone with Mrs Allen! Ugh! Apparently, Mrs Allen was quite the expert on modelling and children's careers (having had *so* much experience with adorable Olivia as a baby), and my mum was fired up with information and plans.

"So if you're interested, I thought it would be good practise, and you could go in with them tomorrow and kind of do a dry run for something that doesn't really count, you know?"

"Wait, you and Mrs Allen are all buddy-buddy now, and you want me to go on an open call with *Olivia*?" I spluttered. I couldn't believe it. From not wanting me to model to now shoving me out on any old call. "Mum!"

She looked at me as if really seeing me for the first time, and then she sat down heavily in a chair at the kitchen table and put her head in her hands. "Oh, dear. I can't believe it. Just listen to me! I'm turning into what I promised myself not to become – a stage mother!" She lifted her head and looked at me with a smile. "Sweetheart, do whatever you like. Mrs Allen just got me all whipped up, but honestly, it's none of my business. If you'd like to go, you should go. If not, don't. It's totally up to you." She shook her head as if to clear it and then stood up to make a cup of coffee.

Now it was my turn to sit at the kitchen table. *Would* it be good practise? *Should* I do it? It might be better than going alone the first time. But spending a day with Olivia Allen? That sounded insane. And what would my friends say? I rested my chin on my hand and thought.

We didn't have any cupcake plans for the next day. I could knock off a lot of my homework tonight. Plus, Mona didn't need me tomorrow. I would be sleeping at Mia's tomorrow night, but I'd be back in time for that. I could actually do it.

"Okay," I said quietly.

"What, sweetheart?" asked my mum, nibbling on a cookie.

"I'll go."

"Oh, Emmy, you don't have to do it on my account. I was a blithering idiot when you came in here. Mrs Allen talks so fast and got me so amped up. Really, you don't have to go."

"No, I think it's a good idea. Look, they at least have some kind of experience, and it might be less scary than going on my own the first time. I'll go."

My mum eyed me warily. "You're sure?"

I nodded. "Yup."

And that's how I ended up on the train to the city the next morning, with Olivia and her mum, after I'd made my weekly delivery of minis to Mona.

Mrs Allen was friendly, but very hyper and wired. She had this big bag filled with snacks and activities and all sorts of grooming supplies. Once my mother had called her last night to say I'd "love to join them" (overstatement), she had e-mailed my mother the open call description, as well as instructions on what I should wear and how I should be styled. It was superorganised and generous, but there was something a little "compulsive" about it, to use my mum's word.

Olivia was actually unusually nice, but kind of quiet. I think her own mum scared her a little, which was sad. She was much better one-on-one than when she was trying to impress her cronies. We chatted on the way in about famous models and their careers, and fashions we liked (I'm not all that into fashion, but thanks to Mia, I can fake it for a while). I told them about the Cupcake Club, and Mrs Allen looked very impressed.

"Why don't *you* start a business like that?" she said to Olivia, but her voice had a little bit of an edge to it, and Olivia winced. I looked away and pretended I hadn't noticed.

The open call was at a big loft downtown in kind of a desolate neighbourhood. They were looking for models for *Teen Look* magazine, which was major. Inside, the loft was packed with girls our age, and we had to sign in at a desk and take numbers. We'd be seen in groups of three, and luckily, Olivia and I were in the same group. Just seeing all these kids was really intimidating. I knew there'd be no way they'd pick me from all this competition, but I knew it would be a good experience. We settled onto a bench to wait, and Olivia's mum pulled out some magazines and handed them to us. I was impressed that she had thought to pack something to pass the time.

Olivia and I chatted a little bit, but then fell silent, just watching the crowd around us. It was better than a reality TV show. There were girls of all shapes, sizes and colours, and a wide range of prettiness, if you ask me. And the mothers! I was so glad my mum wasn't there to witness it, because

I think she would have made me quit then and there.

The mothers were yanking their daughters' hair with hairbrushes, painting on makeup, adjusting the girls' clothing, roughly grasping and maneuvering them. It was like the mothers were taking out their nerves on the daughters. I didn't know where to look.

The people running the tryout were calling in groups of girls, but it was still moving very slowly. Olivia and I sat for two hours before they even got close to our number. We mostly observed and made quiet comments to each other now and then. Olivia was pretty good company. Not too braggy without an audience, and nice enough. We didn't click completely, so I doubted we'd ever really be friends, but she was perfectly pleasant.

From the minute we got there, Mrs Allen was in her element, chatting with all the other mums in various degrees of annoyance about "the biz," as she called it. Everyone had advice and inside information, and it was all delivered with so much urgency, it was making me nervous. She only seemed to notice us occasionally and handed out some dried apricots and seltzer water to keep up our energy, but other than that, it was like we weren't even with her.

Finally, finally, our group was called, and Olivia's mum snapped to attention; brushed Olivia's hair one last time; grabbed her by the shoulders; squatted down to look at her, eye to eye; and said one word: "Sparkle." Then she swatted Olivia on the bum, gave me kind of a closed-mouth smile, and in we went, with one other girl.

Inside the room was a long table filled with grown-ups. They asked for our names and ages and our representation. I could see they were impressed when I said, "Alana Swenson." Two of them looked at each other and nodded, and a third raised his eyebrows really high and made a note on his clipboard. The other girl mentioned another agency. I felt bad for Olivia when she said, "Self-representation for now," so I pretended not to hear.

Olivia went first. They had her stand in front of a white sheet and take some test photos. They called out the poses to her, and she did them naturally, like she'd been doing this all her life: "Three-quarter turn, profile, smile, serious . . ." And then they said, "Thank you! We'll be in touch!" and she was sent out the door. The whole thing took about two minutes.

The other girl went next, and they did the same. Then it was my turn.

"Emma," said one of the women at the table. "How old are you? Where are you from? Do you play any sports? Can you sing?" and all kinds of questions like that. They took lots of photos of me, and it took almost three times as long as it had for the others. At the end they said, "We'll call you with the details of the shoot on Monday." And someone gave me a business card, and then I was out the door too.

Outside, Mrs Allen was packing up, and Olivia was watching the door anxiously. I was pretty sure I'd been picked, but I didn't know the lingo or anything, so I wasn't sure what to tell the Allens.

But I guess because I'd been in there so long, Mrs Allen already knew.

She gave me another tight-lipped smile and said, "All finished finally?" I wanted to say, "No, I have to go off to the shoot now," but I didn't, of course. The Allens had been nice to take me, and I felt bad by how it had worked out. Olivia hadn't been picked, and I was pretty sure I had. I shoved the business card deep into the pocket of my white jeans and knew I wouldn't look at it until I was home.

We had a quiet taxi ride to the station, but when we got to our seats on the train, Olivia's mum had a slew of things to say to Olivia, like, "Were you relaxed? Did you smile? I mean, did you *really* smile, and *sparkle*, like I told you? Because they can tell when you don't really want it. I mean, the camera doesn't miss anything, Olivia."

Olivia took it in silence for a few minutes, but then she burst out, "Jeez, Mum, I did my best! What else do you want from me?"

"I want you to try. That's all. If you'd only apply yourself, and just stick to things . . . You just need a work ethic. Look at Emma, with her cupcake business, and now this . . ."

Olivia looked out the window, and I excused myself to go to the bathroom. I couldn't just sit there and listen. I felt terrible for Olivia.

After that, it was a quiet ride home. I mostly stared out the window of the train. No magazines or apricots were offered, to me or to Olivia, and I was bored and hungry. I couldn't wait to get away from the Allens.

I'd never looked forward to seeing my mum so much in my life.

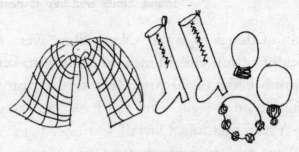

CHAPTER 9

Acting Natural

At school on Monday, I ran into Olivia first thing. She was with her crew, of course: Maggie, Callie and Bella.

Olivia was all smiles. "Hey, I have a really good feeling about that open call on Saturday, you know?" she said loud enough for everyone to hear.

I stared at her for a minute. *Is she kidding?* They hadn't given her one scrap of encouragement. But no, she was serious.

"Yeah. Right. Well, we'll see, I guess!" I said, trying to be cheerful.

She crossed her fingers and waved them in the air at me. I did the same back and went on my way. Weird.

But that evening, when my mum listened to

the messages on our voice mail, there was a call inviting me in for a shoot on Saturday! It would be three hours, and they'd pay me a thousand dollars.

My mum and I whooped and high-fived. But then she said, "Wait, do you want to go? It's for *Teen Look*, right? Is that interesting to you?"

"Mum, who cares?!" I said. "It's a thousand dollars!"

We fell silent and stared at each other. Then we started laughing again. "Oh my goodness!" said my mother, wiping her eyes. "That's a lot of money!"

Suddenly I remembered something. "Wait, but I have my cupcake shoot in the city the same day!"

My mum's eyebrows knit together in concern. "Can we do both? What's the schedule for the cup-cake shoot? This one is from nine to twelve."

I quickly called Mia and discovered our cup-cake shoot was for the afternoon, from one to five p.m. and I told her I'd get back to her with a plan. When I called back later, she proposed we all drive in together and they come to watch my shoot. I agreed, saying my mum would check to see if they could watch, but they could certainly drive in with us, and it was all settled.

97

❖

On Wednesday we had an official meeting of the Cupcake Club, and it felt good to be back. We'd all been a little busy lately – Alexis with our web design, Mia and Katie with school, and me with the modelling stuff – so the cupcake business had slid a little. Except for our weekly delivery to Mona and our big plan for her Jaden Sacks launch party the following Saturday, we didn't have any other jobs booked right now.

"It's okay," I said. "Sometimes it's slow, but just think about the times we've been swamped and how we'd wished it would quiet down. It will pick back up again. I'm sure of it."

Alexis nodded. "We just have to use this quiet time for business development. The website will be great. I can't wait to show you what I have so far." She flipped open her laptop and proceeded to walk us through the site layout.

"And here's where our portfolio will go," she said, "and here would be a photo of us . . ."

"Oh, my dad has great shots from that day. I'll e-mail you some, and you can pick the one for there, okay?"

"Great." Alexis nodded again.

After the site tour, we made our shopping list for

the supplies for Saturday, then divided it up, since we had so much to get. We agreed to meet after school on Friday at my house to pack everything up and do our baking for Mona and the cupcakes for the shoot, then everything would be ready to load in my mum's minivan the next morning. Leaving our meeting, we all felt organised and efficient. It was a good feeling.

At home, my mum had three new messages about go-sees from Alana! One was tomorrow, one was after school next Wednesday, and the other was next Saturday – during the Jaden Sacks launch! And, of course, that go-see was the biggest one. It was for Icon, one of my favourite stores. The money they were offering was insane (five thousand dollars!!!), and my mum and I just stared at each other, dumbfounded. How could people make so much money just standing around having their picture taken?

"But I can't go," I said, coming back down to Earth.

"Emma, that's a lot of money to turn down," my mother said. "Are you sure?"

"I promised Mona two weeks ago. It's a really big day for her. I can't back out now!"

"Could you have someone else go to Mona's

99

in your place? Like Olivia Allen?" my mum suggested.

"No. No way. I owe it to Mona." I felt very strongly about this, as hard as it was to turn down the Icon shoot. Plus, to be honest, there was no way I was going to even suggest Olivia take my place at my beloved The Special Day.

"Well, that's too bad. But you *are* doing the right thing. I know."

We sat quietly for a minute.

"Now, I just need to figure out the logistics of getting you into the city tomorrow for this go-see!" said my mum.

Oh boy. "Sorry," I said. "We don't have to go. It's such short notice."

"No, I think we should, especially since the Icon one won't work out. We don't want Alana to think you're not interested. I can make it work. I'll just have Jake go to the Smiths after school. Dad can organise dinner," said my mum, thinking out loud. "Matt can come home alone. Sam's working . . ."

I guess there's more to modelling than just standing around in front of the camera after all.

The next day, my mum and I drove into the city because, even though parking is expensive, it would allow us to leave as soon as we were done rather than waiting for a train.

The go-see was at a studio in Chelsea, and it was very professional. They'd told me to come dressed like a typical junior high kid (well, that was easy) and to bring my portfolio (my dad had gotten it made at Staples, with big printouts of the photos he'd taken). We were one of the first to arrive, which was lucky, because about fifty more girls filed in after me, and I knew some of them would be here for hours. My mum was asking me all sorts of questions since I'd done this once before. It was kind of funny to have a role reversal where I was experienced at something and she was clueless. She seemed more nervous than I was! After about twenty minutes of sitting there with all the other girls scoping me out, I began to get a little nervous too.

I was called fourth, and my mum came in with me. We introduced ourselves and gave our representation info, and Alana's name again drew impressed looks of approval from the three people sitting on a long sofa against the wall. But no one said anything. I stood there feeling superawkward as they just stared at me, and finally I just looked away and pretended I wasn't there.

After a minute that felt like an eternity, the photographer and his assistant called me over and asked me to stand on the backdrop. Then they had me do the usual poses, which took about two minutes. Then the photographer thanked me. The people on the sofa still hadn't said anything.

I stood for a second. Was that it? Three whole minutes? My mum looked at me uncertainly.

"Thank you! Next!" called the photographer. And we were out the door again, portfolio in hand.

"Well, that was fast," my mother said as we put our jackets on in the elevator.

"Yeah. Kind of weird."

"Was that how it was last time?" she asked.

"No. They asked questions and everything. They actually talked."

"Maybe you just don't have the look they need for this."

"Yeah," I said.

We fell silent.

"You sure you want to keep doing this?" she asked finally.

I nodded. "For now."

"Okay . . ." And we walked back to the parking garage, and went home.

✿

Saturday morning was chaos at our house, and early. I was tired. All this running around was catching up with me, and all I wanted to do was relax in front of the TV, but I had a huge day ahead of me.

The Cupcake Club had shopped, organised, and baked the night before, and I'd got up early today to shower and blow-dry my hair. I'd been told to dress as I normally would, so that was easy, and I was ready when the Cupcakers arrived at seven. We'd have to drop the minis at Mona's on the way into the city, and then my mum would drop me and the Cupcakers at my shoot while she parked.

There was a lot to load into the car, and in the end, we had to sacrifice the tiered wedding cupcake stand that we were planning to use for the Jaden Sacks launch. We'd just have to shoot that next weekend at the event instead.

Luckily, everything went according to plan, and we made it to the *Teen Look* studio with only a few minutes to spare.

I checked in at the front desk and they escorted us back to the studio. Mia was in her element, drinking it all in – the editorial offices, the framed covers on the wall, the racks of clothing samples in the halls – and Alexis was buzzing happily in such a busy work environment. Katie was wide-eyed, saying, "I can't believe I'm at *Teen Look*!" I had to giggle.

Polly, the lady running the shoot, was nice and superstylish. She had masses of long, dark ringlets, and was dressed from head to toe in black, including towering black platform boots that would have been impossible for me to walk in. The bracelets on her arm went *clackity-clack*, and her earrings went *jingledy-jing*, and she smelled amazing, like a cloud of flowers was following her.

She introduced me to the photographer and the stylists, who were all supernice and friendly, and she showed me the buffet, which was all laid out with bagels and spreads and fruit salad and juice. She told the Cupcakers to help themselves too, which was generous. All I could think of when I saw the buffet was Olivia and how she'd love to be here. I felt bad right then, but not for long, because I was quickly whisked off to change into my first look by a stylist named Shoshana.

I waved at my friends and they waved back, their mouths stuffed with breakfast foods. Still smiling, I opened the dressing room and came face-to-face with the ugliest, weirdest outfit I have ever seen.

It was hanging on a mannequin, and it was made up of so many elements, all I could think was that it would look better on a hobo lost in the Arctic Circle.

There were thin, brown leather pants, with a kind of raw edging that looked like an Inuit had sewn them in a rush (we learned about Inuits in social studies last year; they live in the Arctic and dress in heavy stuff, so you can just imagine). There was a grey cotton waffle undershirt that was ripped and distressed; with a plaid button-down overshirt in silk; a big shaggy vest made of fake white fur; a huge orange fur hat; gigantic platform Ugg-type boots; and masses of necklaces made of wooden and glass beads.

"Wow!" I said. "Is that for me?"

"Yes, isn't it amazing? It's from Slim Adkins's new line. It's genius. People are raving about it," said Shoshana.

"Really," I said. I was thinking more of getting sick about it. It all looked pretty heavy. It was a lot of fake animals for one person to carry on her body.

"Yes, let me just break it down so you can get started."

Shoshana took the look apart and began handing me the pieces. I never change in front of people; I just feel insecure about it, so I stood there and waited for her to finish.

"Do you need something?" she asked, stopping what she was doing.

"No." I was confused. *Why?* I wondered.

"Okay, then get going! We only have Miles until noon, so we've got to make the most of it. He costs a fortune."

"Wait . . . You want me to change *now*? *Here?*"

Shoshana looked at me like I was insane. "As opposed to where?" she asked, suddenly not as nice as before.

I felt myself blushing a deep red and was furious at myself. "Oh. Okay. Usually I have privacy when I change," I said. I was proud of myself for saying it, but I was beginning to shake a little with nerves.

"O–kaaay . . . A little unusual for a model to want privacy, but whatever . . ." I could tell she was annoyed, and I was embarrassed. She rushed off all the clothes from the mannequin and kind of flung them at me. "Call me when you're decent," she said, rolling her eyes and then stepping out.

"Thanks," I said, wanting to cry. I got on the pants and the waffle shirt as fast as I could, then I called "Ready," and Shoshana came back in.

It took another ten minutes to get everything on, and then she rushed me out to the hair and makeup lady. That took another half an hour, and

I knew my friends must be getting restless. Finally, I was ready, and they sent me back into the studio.

My mother had arrived from parking the car, and when she saw what I was wearing, her eyes widened in horror, but she didn't say anything. I think she would have said it was not age appropriate, but honestly, I'm not sure how old you'd have to be to pull off this look. I could hear my friends suck in their breath. I looked like a freak. They'd put red eye makeup on my eyelids, up to my brow bones, and made my skin really shiny. I had white lips and my hair had been waxed into dreadlocks that dangled out from under the fur hat. I had to take baby steps or I'd fall over in the boots, and the trousers were actually supertight on me.

But at last I was in front of the camera. The music was thumping, the lights were hot, and my friends were watching. It was all pretty uncomfortable.

Miles started asking for poses, and I was going along with it, but I felt so weird and stiff and so not like myself that I knew I wasn't photographing well. He kept saying, "Okay, relax. Just shake it out. There we go. Okay, I won't bite you! Don't worry," and stuff like that, but I just couldn't get into it. "Okay, Emma, let's just get a real, genuine, relaxed smile. We just need one for the keeper!" It started to be embarrassing, and I could sense he was losing patience but trying to be polite.

Finally, after about twenty agonising minutes, he stepped away from the camera and went to look at the computer to see what he'd got so far. Then he called over Polly, and they went out of the room to chat.

In the meantime the Cupcakers were silent, just watching me. And so was my mum. I could sense they were all worried about me and feeling bad, which made me feel worse.

Finally, Polly came in, all businesslike, and said, "Miles is taking a quick break. I think we'll try one more look, something a little less out there, and see how it goes."

So back I went to try on something else. But this time, though it wasn't all dead (fake) animals, I thought it was even *more* out there. They put me in a sparkly miniskirt, a bathing suit kind of a top, leg warmers, a cape and chunky heels. I looked like Wonder Woman on Halloween. They changed the eye shadow to blue and teased my hair up huge. This time, when I went back into the studio, my friends laughed in surprise. I had to giggle too.

Miles came back in, and he began shooting. But

my giggles wouldn't go away. I don't know if it was nerves, or because my friends were there, or because I knew I'd already blown this job, but I could not stop laughing.

"Glad you're having a good time, now," said Miles at first. "Okay, a few serious shots, then." But I couldn't do it. By this point I was laughing so hard, I was almost crying, and I think that given the chance, I might actually cry. "Okay, Emma, I just need a real, genuine smile. Just for for the keeper shot!" But I just couldn't do anything but giggle. Oh no! Miles and Polly conferenced again, and Polly came over with a look of regret.

"I'm so sorry, Emma, but I think this just isn't going to work today. We love your look, but maybe another time, when you're a little more experienced."

"I am so sorry," I said. "I just—"

She put an arm around me and gave me a little sideways squeeze. "It's okay. It's hard to start at the top. We'll get you again later, when you're a little more seasoned."

"Thanks. Really, I am sorry. And you were so nice."

"You should see how some girls come in here," said Polly, walking me back to the changing room.

"Some are spoiled brats with terrible attitudes, some are exhausted from partying all night, or worse, still partying. It's refreshing to have to deal with inexperience!" She laughed. "Thanks for coming. We'll send you a kill fee if we don't end up using any of the photos."

"Thanks." I stuck out my hand for her to shake, and Polly looked pleasantly surprised.

"Great meeting you," she said.

"Same," I agreed. And then sulky Shoshana helped me undress in silent disapproval, leaving automatically when I got down to the bathing suit.

Back in my normal clothes, I thanked everyone and grabbed some baby wipes from the makeup bench to remove my makeup. There wasn't much I could do about my hair, though.

I went back out to the studio to grab my mum and my friends, but they had already left and were waiting for me back in reception.

"Let's go! Quick!" I said, feeling like I was making a narrow escape.

They dashed after me, giggling, and we fled out onto the street in relief. I was laughing again, hard, but inside I was horrified by how badly I'd blown the job. I cringed thinking of how Polly would call

Alana, and Alana would fire me as her client, and it would be awful.

But maybe not that awful. This business was hard, and I could see a little bit of why the models got paid so much.

You spend a lot of time and energy, all to be poked, prodded and evaluated. You have to get to places at a moment's notice and have the look down right. You have to deliver punctuality, professionalism, courtesy, all with a pleasant attitude. You have to be healthy and strong and fit and have a certain look, as well as no modesty or sense of privacy whatsoever. It was a lot, and I was glad to be done with it for the day.

"Let's discuss all this later, okay?" my mum whispered as my friends chatted away. Thinking of Mrs Allen and her public reprimands of Olivia, I was grateful and nodded.

My friends used my mum's hairbrush to get my hair back down to normal, and then we set out to grab a quick bite of lunch before our next appointment. None of my friends said anything else about the *Teen Look* shoot, and for that I was also grateful.

CHAPTER 10

Model Cupcakes

By the time we hauled everything from the mini-van up to the food stylist's studio, it was just before one o'clock. The stylist met us at the door, and we introduced ourselves. Her name was Debbie, and she was older, like a grandma, and a little chubby, with short grey curls, a huge smile and dimples in her pink cheeks. Her studio was quiet and old-fashioned looking, with brick walls, a big open kitchen that had vintage appliances and a big marble island in the middle of it, and soft-looking wooden floorboards. There was a fireplace off to the side, with a comfy old table and mismatched chairs around it, and classical music was playing over the sound system. She directed us to where to put our supplies, and she offered everyone hot chocolate, which we all accepted, even my mother.

While my mum talked to Debbie about how she'd opened this studio and what other kinds of work she did, we unpacked everything and laid it all out. Then it was time to start.

"Okay," said Debbie, handing around the mugs of cocoa, "the first thing we do is create our shot list, with a brief on each shot. I think you're planning ten shots, right?"

Alexis nodded. She's our natural leader on Cupcake Club business. "Yes. I've written down the cupcakes' names, and we can do them in any order. We did cut one at the last minute because we couldn't fit the display in the car . . ."

We all giggled, and Debbie smiled. "Well, maybe we can figure out something else to show it on." She looked over the list, and then she said, "Okay. Let's go to the cupboard and pick out some pretty plates and napkins and background colour sheets. I think we want to mix it up a little, so we'll shoot maybe half of them in the natural light that's about to start coming in over by the window, and the rest here on the counter with my task lighting. Why don't we have each of you, including your mum, choose one cupcake and pick out a background and props for it, then we'll line it all up on the counter and regroup."

This was going to be fun!

Katie was in ecstasy, looking at all the great kitchen props. I couldn't stop drooling over the top-of-the-line KitchenAid mixer, and I could tell by the gleam in Alexis's eye that she was calculating how much money could be made in a business like this!

We made our selections and created little piles, then we worked on index cards for each shot, listing the props, the cupcake name and whether it would be natural or stage lighting, and what colour background.

Debbie chatted with us the whole time, telling us all the old-fashioned tricks of food styling, like how they used to use Elmer's Glue instead of milk in cereal bowls for cereal ads, and how they don't really cook meat but brown it with a blowtorch, and how ice cream in ads is really just a mix of lard and sugar, so it won't melt under the hot lights. Meanwhile, we each built our cupcake presentations. (My mum needed some guidance on hers, but she managed to pull it off in the end, saying she had a new appreciation for how hard we worked in the Cupcake Club!).

Debbie surveyed the cupcakes, telling us they

were beautiful and explaining that when there were multiples to choose from, the chosen food item is known as the "hero," because it's the one that gets shot. She also instructed us to add some height to the cupcakes whenever possible, because height makes things more interesting in photos. Then she explained how she'd be spraying the cupcakes with cooking spray, to make them shinier, and shooting them at an angle, with the cupcakes filling the frame whenever possible.

Finally, it was time to shoot.

Debbie set up the shots quickly, but then she must've looked through her camera lens a hundred times before pushing the button to shoot. She'd go back and forth, adjusting the lighting, the angle, the background, using tweezers and other little tools to shape and prop and generally primp the cupcakes.

"It's like you this morning, Emma!" said Alexis, laughing as Debbie shot a multicoloured cupcake with a tall heap of rainbow frosting on top. "We're shooting a portfolio, and this cupcake is our little model!"

"Yeah, with the teased hair and everything!" I agreed.

"That was ridiculous," said Mia, with scorn in her voice. "No one dresses like that."

It was easier to talk about it this way while we were working and no one was actually looking at me.

"Did you like any part of that, Emma?" asked Katie.

I could feel my mum waiting for my reply. "I would have liked it better if the clothes weren't so weird. The money is great, but I probably won't get much of it for today," I admitted, then added, "And my agent might fire me."

"Then she doesn't deserve you!" said Alexis sharply.

Tears pricked at my eyes. I loved my friends. And I loved being in business with them. The Cupcake Club was hard work, but it was fun, and we were a team. Modelling was a lonely business. And I had to wonder, Was it appealing just for my ego, so I could say I was a model? Did I need money that badly? Did I even enjoy it? So far, the answers weren't good enough. I'd really need to think hard about it this week.

Our afternoon was cheerful, relaxing and productive, especially compared to my morning. Debbie got so many beautiful shots, I actually thought Alexis might cry. At the end, Debbie promised to e-mail the best shots to Alexis, and we signed a release allowing Debbie to use the shots for publicity and on her website. (She said she'd give us credit, and we said we'd do the same.) Then we packed up, cleaned up and headed home.

I actually fell asleep in the car on the way home and didn't wake up until our first stop to drop off Alexis. By the time we'd dropped off everyone, I was refreshed.

"Thanks, Mum, for everything today," I said from the backseat.

She looked in the rearview mirror. "It was a pleasure. I adore your friends, and I am so impressed by how hard you all worked and what a great team you are."

"It kind of stank, this morning . . ." I wanted to discuss it, but I didn't know what to say.

My mum pressed her lips together. "That just wasn't a good match. I'll have to speak to Alana about it. If you want to keep doing this, that is."

"I think so . . ." I wasn't as sure as I had been. I didn't know if I wanted to stay in just to prove something or if I actually liked it.

"If that's the case, then you *will* have to be more professional. Maybe you could take some classes or something," said my mum. "I also think it's a mistake to bring your friends. We certainly won't do that again."

"We kind of owe Olivia one, though . . ." I said, feeling guilty.

"Of course. But that's different. She isn't there to giggle with."

I thought of Olivia's mum and her "sparkle" directive. "That's for sure," I agreed, and sighed.

Back home, there were three messages from Alana, asking my mum to call her.

"Uh-oh," I said, listening to the third one.

My mum grimaced, and dialled. "Alana?"

Boy, she must've picked up on the first ring. I braced myself, waiting to hear shouting through the phone. I tried to read my mum's expression, to see if I could tell what Alana was saying. Finally, my mum got a word in edgewise.

"It's not your fault. No, don't be silly. She's fine." My mum looked up at me, smiling and making a surprised face. "Well, yes, the outfits were inappropriate, but Polly was very nice. No, don't worry about it. Please. Whatever money you can get is fine. Thanks. Talk soon. Bye."

My mum hung up the phone and stared at it in shock for a second before looking up at me. "Alana was furious. At *them*! Polly called her to explain what happened, and Alana freaked out that they'd taken a child and tried to dress her as an adult, and on and on. She wanted to know if you were 'scarred for life' and insisted she will get every penny of the original fee for you. Wow!"

I grinned. "No wonder people are impressed when they hear she's my agent. She's fierce!"

"We're lucky," said my mum. "Now let's make sure we deserve her."

For Wednesday's go-see, my mum learned that it was an open call, so she made me invite Olivia, who was thrilled. Ugh. Even worse, my mum had no one to pawn Jake off on, so he had to come too!

We took the train into the city, and the call was at a big casting company's office. There were all sorts of commercials and ads being cast at once, so there were hordes of kids in different staging areas. It was overwhelming. One whole group was dressed as elves, which was kind of funny, and another was all in ballerina outfits. I felt like I was in a dream.

Olivia and I got our call numbers and studio assignment, and my mum and Jake tagged along to the holding area. It wasn't that big of a group waiting, and I didn't understand why until the door opened at one point and I got a flash of what was inside. Dogs. Lots of them! I suddenly feel great, because I am a dog expert! If this job calls for working with dogs, I have already nailed it!

I smiled at Olivia. "Dogs," I said confidently.

"What?" she asked, a look of fear creeping over her face.

"It must be a dog food ad or something. There are tons of dogs in there!" I announced happily.

Olivia paled and sank down into her chair. "I hate dogs," she whispered. "I'm afraid of them!"

And sure enough, when we're called and ushered in, the room was alive with pooches. I dropped to my knees to play with the first ones to come to me, but Olivia backed up against a wall, terrified. Jake followed me into the room and got down on his knees too, laughing hysterically when the dogs began to lick his face. My mum signed us in and sat on a chair to wait for our test shots.

Olivia was called first. She inched up to the backdrop, and a handler brought some dogs over to her on leashes. I could see that she was trying not to look scared, but it was not working.

"Okay, just smile and relax, please," said the photographer.

But as I watched, Olivia could not relax and she could not smile. After, like, three shots the ad person said to Olivia, "Okay, thank you!" Olivia looked stunned that she was already done. "Thanks!" the lady said again when Olivia wasn't fast enough to move off the backdrop.

"That's it?" Olivia asked as she walked off.

"Uh-huh. Next?" the lady suddenly called, and I stepped in.

She handed me the dogs' leashes and asked for a pose, but I was distracted by the animals that wouldn't seem to do as I said. They were pulling me one way, while the photographer was in the other direction, and suddenly I felt something warm on my leg. No! A dachshund just peed on me!

"Sorry! Thank you!" the agency lady said, and now I'm hustled off the backdrop and handed a wad of paper towels. *What?* This was my moment to shine! Dogs loved me! But it was not to be.

I mopped my leg and noticed the ad lady and the photographer conferring for a minute. Then the ad lady went over to my mum, and they chatted briefly. My mum called over Jake from where he was wrestling with a bunch of dogs, and I am mortified. Here we were, unprofessional on the shoot again. This time I'm sure they'll call Alana and then she'll fire me. *Why does Jake always have to ruin everything?* I thought angrily.

But suddenly Jake was shrugging, and they were changing his shirt. He was on the backdrop laughing with a bunch of adorable golden retriever puppies rolling all over him, and they were taking his picture. Olivia and I stood in shock, watching, as Jake nailed the job we'd both come in for.

By the time we were on the train back to Maple Grove, Olivia and I were in stitches, laughing over being upstaged by a little boy with no front teeth, and my mum was moaning about having two models in the family. Jake was clueless about what it all meant. He just had fun playing with the doggies, and he said he didn't mind if his picture ended up in a magazine!

The night ended with me thinking maybe it would be better if I left the modelling career to Jake, who seemed to take it all pretty lightly.

CHAPTER II

Jaden Sacks!

Mona called me in a complete panic on Thursday afternoon.

"Darling! I'm in a pinch! Jaden Sacks wants oodles of bridesmaids at the launch, and I've only signed up you! Help! I need some more gorgeous tweenagers!"

I laughed. "How about the Cupcake Club, since they're already planning on coming? At least I know they're free!"

"Sounds great to me, but would you be able to send me a photo? Jaden Sacks's publicity team likes to approve the models in advance, to make sure they're consistent with the company image. Not too flashy, you know?"

"Sure. I just happen to have a great photo."

We hung up, and I e-mailed Mona the link to our new demo website. In the section About Us, there's a really pretty and fun group shot from the session with my dad. An hour later, Mona called back. "Book them, darling! They're approved!"

But that night, as I was lying down to go to sleep, my stomach dropped.

Olivia!

I should have invited her too. I didn't want to, but I kept thinking about her mum, and I kind of felt bad for her. Going on all those casting calls is tough for anyone. It would be a nice thing to do.

I climbed out of bed, switched on my light and laptop, and dashed off a quick, kind of neutral e-mail to Olivia, asking if she could e-mail me a head shot, since I might know of a job for her. Of course it was in my in-box first thing the next morning when I checked, and I forwarded it to Mona with the subject line "One More" and crossed my fingers.

At school, Olivia accosted me, again in front of her friends, asking me about the job we're booking and have I heard back about the dog food one yet. Her gang was all ears, impressed.

I tried to make it sound like she had a chance

for the dog food one, which was a flat-out lie, and I prayed that Jaden Sacks didn't like her look. I was a little mad that I had tried to do something nice and she was just acting like regular Olivia.

It turned out, though, that Jaden Sacks thought Olivia was, according to Mona, "just divine." If she only knew.

On Saturday, as Icon's five thousand dollars sat in their bank account rather than my pocket, we all trooped over to The Special Day, cupcakes and tiered stand in hand. My dad drove us, because he said my mum has seen more of me lately than he did, and he wanted to grab some snapshots of the big day, anyway.

Mona and Patricia and their team were even more aflutter than I've ever seen, and all the furniture in the store had been pushed against the walls, to make room for the crowds. Olivia was there waiting for us with her mother, and between the two of them, it was hard to tell who was more ecstatic. I felt good about calling and including her after all, mostly because it might make her mum a little nicer to her.

We scrambled inside; set up the huge cupcake display, which Mona swooned over; and then headed back to have our hair done. Mona hired a professional hair stylist for the day, and we all lined up to be lightly worked over by the curling iron.

Then Patricia whisked us away for our look lineup. I retrieved my slip from its usual hanging spot and put on my first dress. It was a floaty, linen dress, with just a tiny bit of stitched detail at the hem, and a wide, pink sash. I loved it. It could not be more comfortable to wear, and pretty! It was something I would have picked out for myself. As Patricia finished tying a big bow in the back, I slipped on white ballet slippers and headed out to show my dad.

But when I got out to the main salon, I saw him chatting with Mona and another woman I didn't recognise. I started to approach them, and then Mona spied me and waved me over, calling, "Darling, come!"

"Darling! Isn't she divine?" she said to the other woman. "This . . . is Jaden Sacks!"

"Oh! Oh my gosh! Hi! Wow! It is so cool to meet you! I'm just . . . I love, love, love your dresses! I wish I could wear them every day. Like, even to school!" I knew I sounded silly and I was gushing, but it was all true. Jaden Sacks smiled.

She wasn't as old as I would have thought —
maybe in her late thirties. She had golden hair to
her shoulders, cut in a swingy kind of shag, and she
was tan, with bright blue eyes. She was very petite,
and when I shook her hand, I was surprised by how
light and thin it was. She had real artist's hands —
graceful and delicate. She grinned warmly and her
eyes sparkled, and I felt like we were sharing a great
joke, like we were instantly friends.

"I have a lot to thank you for!" she said, in a
surprisingly girlish voice.

"Me?! Why?"

"Your ad was a huge hit! Our flagship store
got one hundred and seventy-two calls looking for
the dress you wore in that ad. One of the reasons
I was hoping to meet you was to see if you and
Mona would mind if we bought the shot and ran
it nationally."

"What? Really?" I thought of Olivia and her
"national ad" information. "Great. I mean, you'll
have to speak to my agent . . ." I looked around for
my dad.

"Oh my gosh! An agent! They start so young
these days!" Jaden joked. "Who *is* your agent?
You?" She looked at my dad, who was standing
behind me.

But he shook his head. "No, I'm her father. Emma's agent is someone called Alana Swenson."

Jaden put her head in her hands, like she was devastated, but she was joking. "Of course it is. She wouldn't let someone like you escape her radar! I'll call her on Monday. She owes me a lunch, anyway, since we used only Swenson girls at our last runway show!"

"I bet she loved that!" I said, laughing.

"Oh, she did." Jaden laughed back. "Ka-ching!"

Patricia came scurrying up to say the bridal models were all ready and the bridesmaids nearly so and did we want to open the doors yet. I turned to look outside, and there were so many people standing beyond the doors that I couldn't even see past them. Wow! I gulped.

"I'll let you go. Congratulations! See you after!" I said to Jaden. And I scurried back to the dressing room.

Mrs Allen was there, whispering directives to Olivia, but Patricia booted her out, and Olivia relaxed after that. The next half hour went by in a blur as we did our fashion show before a couple hundred people, and then we could relax as we mingled.

The Cupcakers thought the whole thing was

a hoot, but they were exhausted at the end.

"This is really hard work!" said Alexis. "Just being on your feet this long is tiring!"

"Yeah, and all that smiling," said Katie, who seems to be smiling all the time, anyway.

"I loved it!" said Olivia, and it was true. She had seemed happy. Maybe runway work was the thing for her. I wouldn't mind too much if Mona ended up using her too. It might be nice to have a little company at the trunk shows. "Of course, it's nothing like a national ad shoot for TV, when they have all the buffets lined up . . ."

I groaned, and everyone laughed.

Olivia looked up and blushed.

Before we all changed, my dad, who'd been taking pictures all day, asked the Cupcakes to come outside, and he got some great shots of the Cupcake Club with Jaden Sacks and Mona in front of the store.

The pictures turned out so great that when he e-mailed them to Jaden and Mona later, they picked one to run in an ad in the *Gazette*.

A month later my family had a big Sunday dinner to celebrate Jake's dog food ad in the new issue of *Parents' Life* magazine and the full-page ad in the *Gazette* of all the Cupcakers with Mona and Jaden.

The best part was at the bottom of the bridal ad. It said:

jadensacks.com

thespecialdaysalon.com

thecupcakeclub.com

I had dialled back on my modelling career a little by then. My mom had told Alana we'd only do tween stuff, and only on weekends, and only with at least a week's notice. And Alana was fine with that.

Olivia worked a trunk show at Mona's with me one weekend, and it was fun to have her there. She was a lot nicer when she was alone, and she was a lot more relaxed when her mum wasn't around. I could kind of see how Mia liked her at first, and I kind of felt badly that her mum could be so hard on her. We went on our lunch break together, and it was my treat, with money from my last photo shoot. We had apricots and seltzer water from the Fruit & Nut stand, and cupcakes for dessert!

But the next Monday at school, she was back to her old self again. As I walked to my locker, I could hear her talking about the fashion show at Mona's.

"Emma was okay, but anyone could tell she was inexperienced," she was saying. Bella and Callie were hanging on to her every word. "I was the star of the show, if I do say so myself. Everyone was staring at me, and I heard Jaden asking Mona who I was. That's why I wasn't in the print ad. They wanted to save me, so I could do an ad by myself, without being lumped in with all the, well, regular girls. Poor Emma! I'll probably have to replace her at The Special Day, but it was going to happen eventually. She's just not 'model material.'"

I couldn't believe it! After all I had done to try and help her out. I was steaming. I walked right up to her and tapped her on the shoulder. Olivia blinked and looked startled for a moment, but then went right back into her act.

"Oh, Emma, I'm so sorry! I didn't mean for you to hear that," she said. She touched my arm lightly. "But maybe it's better coming from a friend, you know?"

I looked at Bella and Callie, who just stared at me and nodded sadly.

"I think you're right, Olivia," I replied, "that sometimes criticism is better coming from a friend. But you aren't my friend. I tried to do something nice for you after you didn't get booked on any jobs and after Alana Swenson didn't take you on as a client, and I asked Mona to include you in The Special Day event. I'm sorry you weren't in the ad that ran. They were looking for someone less fake-model looking and . . . well, someone with a bit of sparkle."

I felt a little bad right then, because Olivia turned really pale and looked like she wanted the floor to swallow her up. I almost started to say something about being a baby model as her last job, but I stopped. I had said enough to make my point. There was no need to stoop down to her level.

I smiled my best "model" smile and turned to walk down the hall, like it was a big runway. I thought of my mum, who thought I always sparkled no matter what, and I kept walking towards my friends, who didn't care if I was a model or not. I thought of going to The Special Day and putting on the pretty dresses with my friends Mona and Patricia and just having fun. I thought of how excited I was that the Cupcake

Club had booked a bunch of new jobs, thanks to our website. I smiled a real, genuine smile. And then I laughed. Because if Miles was there, I know that smile would have been "the keeper."

Coco Simon always dreamed of opening a cupcake bakery but was afraid she would eat all of the profits. When she's not daydreaming about cupcakes, Coco edits children's books and has written close to one hundred books for children, tweens, and young adults, which is a lot less than the number of cupcakes she's eaten. Cupcake Diaries is the first time Coco has mixed her love of cupcakes with writing.

Still Hungry?

There's always room for another Cupcake!

Katie and the Cupcake Cure

978-0-85707-338-9 £5.99

978-0-85707-402-7

Mia in the Mix

978-0-85707-403-4 £5.99

978-1-86707-404-1

Emma on Thin Icing

978-0-85707-405-8 £5.99

978-1-85707-406-5

Alexis and the Perfect Recipe

978-0-85707-407-2 £5.99

978-1-85707-408-9

Katie, Batter Up!

978-0-85707-883-4 £5.99

978-1-85707-881

Mia's Baker's Dozen

978-0-85707-885-8 £5.99

978-1-85707-886-5

Emma All Stirred Up!

978-1-47111-554-7 £5.99

978-1-47111-555-4

Alexis Cool as a Cupcake

978-1-47111-556-1 £5.99

978-1-47111-557-8

Katie and the Cucpake War

978-1-47111-632-2 £5.99

978-1-47111-633-9

Mia's Boiling Point

978-1-47111-654-6 £5.99

978-1-47111-635-3

Emma, Smile and Say "Cupcake!"

978-1-47111-636-0 £5.99

978-1-47111-637-7

Alexis Gets Frosted

978-1-47111-638-4 £5.99

978-1-47111-639-1

The Cupcake Diaries

Katie
and the
Cupcake Cure

Coco Simon

Katie Brown's school year is not off to a good start. Her best friend has ditched her for the Popular Girls' Club and she's worried that she's going to spend the rest of the year alone. But Katie soon realises that sometimes making new friends can be the icing on the cupcake...

When it comes to a crush, can Alexis stand the heat?

Alexis Becker is the most organised, most prepared-for-everything member of the Cupcake Club. But Alexis has secrets too ... like her messy room, and the biggest secret of all – having a crush! But she's about to learn that there's no perfect recipe for love...

LM
1/14
